Where the Heart Is

Look for these titles by
Ally Blue

Now Available:

Where the Heart Is

Ally Blue

A SAMHAIN PUBLISHING, LTD. publication.

Samhain Publishing, Ltd.
577 Mulberry Street, Suite 1520
Macon, GA 31201
www.samhainpublishing.com

Where the Heart Is
Copyright © 2009 by Ally Blue
Print ISBN: 978-1-60504-425-5
Digital ISBN: 978-1-60504-370-8

Editing by Sasha Knight
Cover by Anne Cain

First Samhain Publishing, Ltd. electronic publication: January 2009
First Samhain Publishing, Ltd. print publication: October 2009

Dedication

To Melanie and Jesse for introducing me to Carrboro, especially Weaver Street Market and The Open Eye. Talk about inspiration! And as always, my eternal gratitude to my wonderful, wonderful critique partners for their support, their friendship and their knack for seeing things I don't.

Chapter One

Carrboro's Weaver Street Market was a veritable Godiva Gold Collection of eye candy. Especially on sunny, unseasonably warm Saturday afternoons in early January. The faint lingering nip in the air wasn't nearly enough to discourage the crowds of aging hippies, families and college students from congregating on the Market's wide lawn and outdoor tables.

Slouched on a bench beneath a spreading oak, legs stretched out in front of him, Dean Delapore lifted his black shades and aimed a smoldering look at the doe-eyed young man watching him from across the shaded lawn. The boy gave him a coy smile.

The bench moved as someone plopped down beside Dean. He turned to face Kerry Shiffer, one of the friends he'd come here to visit. "Did you get your ice cream?"

"It's not ice cream, it's gelato." Fishing in her canvas grocery bag, Kerry pulled out a small brown and white container. "Organic and locally produced by Green Fields Creamery."

"Of course." Dean slid his shades back into place and lifted his face to the winter sunshine. "I'm glad you and

Ron talked me into coming up here to visit. Y'all know how much I love my job, but I seriously needed a vacation. We've been up to our eyeballs in freaky cases lately."

Kerry turned sideways on the bench and tucked a leg underneath her, one hand absently rubbing her six-months-pregnant belly. "Well, we're both glad you could come up. With the baby coming Ron needs to save up his time off, and we both need to hang on to our money. But we wanted to see you. It's been way too long."

"It sure has." Putting an arm around Kerry's shoulders, Dean kissed the top of her curly auburn head. "I miss college some days. The three of us had some great times together here at UNC."

"We sure did." Kerry planted a kiss on Dean's cheek, patted his knee and rose to her feet. "Come on, let's head back now. Ron should be home soon."

"Cool." Dean jumped up and fell into step beside Kerry. "I hate that he had to go in to work today."

She shrugged. "That's what he gets for being the only one there who actually knows how the hell their computer network functions, I guess. At least it's only for a little while."

"Yeah." Sticking his hands in his back pockets, Dean grinned at a gap-toothed little girl who waved at him from atop a nearby brick planter. "I don't blame y'all a bit for settling here. It's a great town. Always has been."

"Yeah. I'm just glad this warm snap hung around for your visit. It's usually colder than this in January." She gave him a sidelong glance as they crossed the street and headed down the hill past colorful shops and restaurants. "I wish you could stay longer."

"Me too. But Bay City Paranormal could only spare me for a couple of weeks."

Kerry wrinkled her freckled nose. "I don't see why they couldn't let you off for longer."

Dean laughed. "Bo was willing to let me off for a month, but I told him I'd only take two weeks. It's a small business, and we've been super busy lately. They need me."

"Yeah, but still—"

"Kerry, I love you, but give it a rest, huh?" Dean nudged Kerry's shoulder. "I don't mind. Really. Like I said, I love my job. And I love my coworkers. They're a great group."

Her round face lit up, blue eyes sparkling. "Any of them you love more than the others?"

Shaking his head, Dean pushed the "walk" button at the next corner. "You know me, Kerry. I don't tie myself down."

She shot him a careful look. "You would have, once. Please tell me she didn't totally destroy your ability to settle down with somebody else."

At that moment, Dean was grateful he had his sunglasses on. He didn't want Kerry to see his eyes, because she was right. Sharon had been his first real love. The first person, male or female, with whom he'd seriously considered having a permanent relationship.

11

When she found out he was bisexual and had slept with men, she'd left him. He didn't like to admit, even to himself, just how painful that had been. Or just how much it had affected his life since.

"I got over Sharon a long time ago," he said softly. "Believe me, if I find Mr. or Ms. Right, what happened with Sharon won't stop me from hanging onto them. I just haven't found that person yet, that's all."

"So it's got to be true love forever, or no deal?"

"What's wrong with that?"

Pursing her lips, Kerry picked at a loose thread on her long red skirt. "Nothing, I guess. It just seems kind of lonely to me."

"I date a lot, I get laid a lot, but I still get my own space with no one telling me I can't have beer and Fritos for breakfast or lay around watching TV in my underwear. That's not lonely, that's the best of both worlds."

He refused to acknowledge the small but growing part of him which longed to wake up every morning with his arms around someone he loved. To spend a lifetime learning that person inside and out. It didn't seem likely to happen, and he saw no point in mourning something he'd probably never have. Especially since it was his own tendency to hold himself back that kept him from having the kind of relationship he wanted.

Kerry frowned at him, but before she could say anything her cell phone trilled. She shot him a "this conversation isn't over" look as she fished the phone out of her purse and flipped it open.

"Hey, babe," she said, eyes sparkling like they always did when she talked to her husband. "We're on our way back from the Market, are you already home?"

Tuning out his friends' conversation, Dean stuck his hands in his back pockets and gazed around him. Just ahead, the town's newest Thai restaurant had its front doors flung open, letting out a spicy, mouthwatering scent. Next door, customers wandered in and out of a bookstore specializing in rare and out-of-print volumes. A wave of lilting violins drifted from the music store across the street.

At the next corner, two young men crossed the street with their arms around each other. The blond tilted up the brunet's face and kissed him. Dean smiled, the sight bringing a mix of conflicting emotions. Mobile, where he'd been born and raised and still lived, wasn't a particularly dangerous place for gays, but neither was it a place where a man could kiss another man in public without any thought to the possible consequences.

Sometimes, he really missed the open and accepting attitudes here in Carrboro and neighboring Chapel Hill.

"Well, crap." Snapping the cell phone closed, Kerry shoved it into her purse. "Ron's not done yet. He's got to stay at work until probably midafternoon."

"Aw, damn."

"He's taking a break right now. He's headed over to The Open Eye. I told him we'd meet him there."

"Cool." Dean glanced at the shopping bag hanging from Kerry's arm. "What about your gelato? It'll melt."

She grinned at him. "We'll go ahead and eat it. It goes great with the organic Sumatran dark roast."

"Awesome." Taking Kerry's hand, Dean led her across the busy street. "Do they still have those chocolate croissants?"

"Uh-huh."

"Fantastic. I haven't had one of those in years."

Laughing, Kerry pushed open the door of Carrboro's most popular coffee shop. Dean shoved his shades up on top of his head and breathed in the heavenly scents of baked goods and fresh-brewed coffee. It was the smell of college mornings spent huddled over the colorful tables with his friends, discussing classes, music, girls or boys they wanted to get into bed. All the things that seemed so important then, with the world at their feet and all their lives ahead of them.

Time had a way of teaching a person what was truly important, Dean reflected as he and Kerry took their place in line. Friends. Family. Partners. If there was one thing Dean had learned in his life, it was that nothing mattered as much as keeping the people he loved close, and letting them know how much they meant to him. He liked to think he lived by that creed, and that his friends and family knew how he treasured them.

He ignored the empty ache inside for a love like Kerry and Ron shared.

Behind him, the rather shrill tinkle of the bell on the door announced an arrival to the shop. A shoulder clipped Dean's as someone rushed past the line and straight to the counter, sending Dean stumbling into Kerry. A woman passing on her other side caught her elbow, narrowly preventing a fall.

"Hey, watch it," Dean called, scowling at the back of the man who'd run into him. "Pregnant lady here, huh? You almost made me knock her over."

The man turned, blinking in surprise as his large brown eyes lit on Kerry. "Kerry? Oh my God I'm sorry! I'm just in kind of a rush, and wasn't looking where..." He stopped, blowing out a breath. One long, slender hand raked through shaggy shoulder-length hair the color of redwood. "Sorry. Listen, y'all come out to my place tonight for karaoke, I'll give you dinner."

Kerry laughed. "We'd love to come for karaoke, but you don't need to feed us."

"But I—"

"You were in a hurry, and you accidentally ran into someone," Kerry finished. "It happens. I'm fine, don't worry about it."

The stranger bit his lower lip, and Dean's breath caught. Something about the nervous action and the uncertain look in those huge, expressive eyes made Dean want to pull the man into his arms and comfort him.

"I'd still love it if you and Ron came for karaoke. Y'all haven't been out for at least a month." His gaze flicked sideways to Dean, then back again, as if he wasn't sure he should speak to him. "And you can bring, um, guests." He darted another look at Dean, this one sizzling with curiosity. "Um, yeah. See you later."

The man turned and leaned against the counter, talking low and fast to the young woman on the other side. Dean stared, admiring the slim, tight lines of the stranger's body. Black jeans hugged long legs and the sweetest ass Dean had seen in ages. A pale blue shirt with the tails hanging out and the sleeves rolled up set off the man's deep red hair and golden skin tone perfectly.

"Who's that?" Dean asked, nudging Kerry's elbow. "He's hot."

Kerry grinned. "How do you do that?"

"Do what?" He tilted his head sideways to better view the curve of buttock and thigh as the man shifted from foot to foot.

"Pick out the gay ones, every time." Kerry slapped him on the butt. "Are you listening?"

"I didn't know he was gay. I just thought he was hot." Dean flashed his friendliest smile as the man turned around and hurried toward the door carrying a large paper bag. The man blushed and looked away, but Dean saw the way the corners of his mouth turned up as he passed. Dean swiveled around to watch the man walk out the door. "Oh yeah. *Smokin'* hot. So who is he?"

Snickering, Kerry stepped up to the counter and ordered two organic Sumatrans before turning back to Dean. "That's Sommer Skye. He's a good friend of mine and Ron's."

Dean laughed. "Sommer Skye? What the hell were his parents thinking?"

"They were serious hippies." Kerry held her hand out.

Dean handed her two dollars, which she gave to the girl behind the counter along with her own money. Taking the change, Kerry picked up the huge indigo mug the clerk handed her and led Dean toward a table containing carafes of soy milk and half-and-half, packets of raw sugar and a small pitcher of honey. "They disappeared four years ago. Nobody's seen or heard a trace of them since. It's kind of a sore spot with Sommer, so do *not* say anything, okay?"

"Cross my heart." Dean stirred honey and a generous amount of half-and-half into his coffee and took a cautious sip from the orange and yellow mug. "Oh man, that's good. So, we're going to his place tonight, huh?"

"Yep." Kerry poured a packet of raw sugar and a dollop of soy milk into her coffee and stirred. "He owns the Blue Skye Inn and Winery just outside town. It's a cool place, you'll love it. He's set up the wine shop and tasting room in the old barn, and he has Karaoke Night there every Saturday. Five bucks a head, and you get one complimentary glass of his chardonnay and as much karaoke as you can handle. Half the town turns out for it, it's a real blast."

"Sounds like it." Dean followed Kerry to a small round table bathed in sunshine pouring through the wall-to-wall windows. As he slid into the chair, he caught sight of a tall, lanky man chaining a bicycle to the rack outside. "Hey, there's Ron."

Kerry's face lit up. She tapped on the window. Ron looked up, smiled and waved at her. She waved back, beaming. Dean chuckled. His friends had been married for seven years, and had dated all through college, but they were still head over heels for each other, and it showed. Dean thought it was adorable.

Ron swung the door open and bounded in, gray eyes shining. Flipping his long golden ponytail over his shoulder, he slid into the chair beside Kerry and put an arm around her. "Hey, babe."

"Hey yourself." She tilted her face up for a kiss. "We're going to Sommer's for karaoke tonight."

"Okay, cool. I'll be home by four, so no problem." Ron's bearded face broke into a wide grin as he leaned over to clap Dean on the shoulder. "He's single, and Kerry says he's cute. Want me to set you up?"

"No need, I can handle it. But thanks anyway." Dean took a sip of his coffee, licking the rich, dark taste from his lips. "By the way, he is beyond cute. He's *gorgeous*. Just so you know."

Ron's eyebrows shot up. "When did you meet him?"

"I didn't. Yet. But I sure am looking forward to it."

"Sommer was in here just before you got here," Kerry explained, answering the puzzled look on her husband's face. "He was in a rush and didn't stay for introductions, but Dean noticed him. Big surprise, I know. I told him we'd come out for karaoke."

Ron chuckled. "Sommer's always in a rush. Was he in here getting coffee beans again?"

"Most likely. I noticed Weaver Street Market was out of that fair trade Mexican blend he serves at the Inn." Kerry glanced at Dean. "He usually gets all his stuff at the

Market, but he comes here for his beans when they're out at Weaver Street."

Dean nodded over his coffee cup. "Very Carrboro of him. I like that in a man."

"You have to try his zinfandel tonight, Dean," Ron said, leaning back in his chair and stretching. "You'll get a free glass of chardonnay, but the zinfandel's out of this world. He'll give you a free taste, if you want."

An array of decidedly impure mental images flashed through Dean's mind. He rested his chin in his hand. "You think he'd give me a free taste of anything else? I promise to ask nicely."

"I'm sure he would. He's got merlot, Pinot Grigio, and—" Ron stopped, his face flushing pink. "Oh. Dean, you have a filthy mind."

"That can't possibly surprise you at this point." Kerry took a long swallow of coffee. "You want me to order you a coffee, hon?"

"Naw, I'll get it." Yawning, Ron rose to his feet. "Y'all want anything else while I'm up?"

"A spoon." Kerry held up her bag. "I have gelato."

"Oh yeah, and I wanted a chocolate croissant. Mr. Hotpants distracted me." Pushing away from the table, Dean stood and dug his wallet out of his pocket. "I'll come with you, Ron."

"Cool." Leaning down, Ron kissed his wife's forehead, then followed Dean to the counter. He shot Dean a keen look. "You look tired. Is everything all right back in Mobile?"

"Yeah, it's fine. The last few months have been kind of…" He trailed off, not knowing quite what to say about all he'd experienced since joining Bay City Paranormal. "It's been weird," he said finally.

"That's what you get when you work for a paranormal investigations agency."

"Yeah, I guess." Dean smiled at his friend. "It's good to be back here. I missed y'all."

"Same here, man." Sweeping Dean into a tight hug, Ron planted a kiss on each cheek. "It's been ages since we got to hang out."

Before Dean could answer, Kerry's voice rang out across the crowded shop. "You guys can make out if you want, but no threesomes. Only wholesome family sex around the baby."

Ron raised his eyebrows. He and Dean cracked up at the same time, along with half the customers in the shop.

Oh yeah, Dean thought as he let go of Ron and waited to place his order. *I've missed these people, and this place.*

Of course, just because Carrboro and Chapel Hill held so much nostalgia for him didn't mean there were no new memories to be made here. With any luck, some of those new memories would involve a slender, dark-eyed inn-and-winery owner between his legs.

He grinned. *Karaoke Night, here I come.*

Chapter Two

"Here we are," Ron announced, guiding the old red Nova into a narrow gravel lane. A wooden sign beside the road spelled out Blue Skye Inn & Winery in deep red letters against a pale blue background. "Wow, it's crowded tonight."

"I'll say. Is it always like this?" Dean gazed around from the backseat, taking it all in. About one hundred yards ahead, the gravel lane expanded into a huge gravel parking area. It was packed with cars. Even the row of bike racks along one side was full. On the far side of the parking lot stood a tremendous wooden structure which had clearly begun life as a barn and been added onto over the years. It was painted sky blue with the name of the business over the entrance in red letters, matching the sign by the road. Light, music and laughter poured from the doorway as patrons entered in a steady stream.

Dean grinned. He liked it already.

Kerry turned in her seat. "It's not usually quite this bad, but it's always busy on Saturday. Karaoke Night's pretty popular."

"I think it's a parents' weekend at the college, or

maybe a game. Something going on at UNC, though, which is probably why it's so crowded." Squinting against the light of the sunset, Ron pointed ahead and to the left. "Babe, is that an empty spot?"

Kerry pulled her sunglasses off and looked where Ron was pointing. "Yeah. It's close to the front too, grab it before someone else does."

Nodding, Ron sped up and eased the Nova into the space. "Dean, you gonna sing for us?"

Dean considered as they all climbed out of the car. "Depends. What do they have?"

"Oh, everything." Ron locked the car door and pocketed the keys. "Classic country, pop hits from the forties to now, show tunes, even some really freaky-ass obscure shit."

Laughing, Kerry slid an arm around her husband's waist as he walked up to her and they joined the throng heading toward the barn. "You remember that song Fish Heads?"

"Yeah, it's on my iPod." Dean widened his eyes at her. "What, you mean they have *that*?"

"They do," Ron said. "Want to duet on that one?"

"Hell yeah." Sticking his hands in his jacket pockets, Dean drew a deep breath. The chilly evening air smelled of grass and sunshine. Behind the barn and to the right, Dean caught sight of a large, Victorian-style farmhouse with a wide covered porch. The white paint glowed orange with the sunset light. "Is that the Inn?" he asked, nodding toward the building.

Kerry nodded. "Yeah. Cute, huh?"

"Mm-hm." Dean slowed to get a good look at the building. "Very romantic looking."

"It's haunted," Ron said, glancing over his shoulder at Dean.

Groaning, Kerry smacked Ron's arm. "You weren't supposed to tell him that, you dork."

An expression of almost comic dismay crossed Ron's face. "Oh, that's right. Oops."

With one last curious glance at the Inn, Dean trotted to catch up with his friends. He gave them both a stern look. "Why would y'all not want to tell me that?"

Kerry took his hand and squeezed it. "I know you, Dean. You're gonna want to know all about the ghosts, and you're gonna want to investigate, even if it's an unofficial investigation. I'm selfish. I don't want to share you while you're here."

Touched, Dean leaned down and planted a kiss on her cheek. "Hey, I came all the way up here to get *away* from work, remember? I'm curious, sure, but I'm not about to let that get in the way of hanging out with y'all."

Kerry smiled. "Good."

When they reached the entrance to the barn, Dean dug a five-dollar bill out of his back pocket and handed it to the smiling middle-aged woman at the door. After checking his ID, she stamped his hand and gave him a dark blue ticket which he was informed was the voucher for his free glass of chardonnay. Thanking her, he followed a plump girl in a Blue Skye polo shirt and jeans across the floor. Kerry and Ron trailed behind, talking quietly.

Tapping the edge of the ticket against his lower lip, Dean gazed around in delight. The room they'd entered was enormous, with a clean-swept floor of rough wooden planks. The only light came from small red-shaded lamps on each table, and the high ceiling was lost in shadows. Antique wine-making equipment sat displayed at intervals along the walls, with little plaques beside them explaining their history and use. Oak barrels with wide, round wooden tops formed the tables at which a variety of people sat sipping wine, laughing and talking. A few of the customers were dressed up, but most wore jeans, sweaters and other casual clothes. Unsurprisingly, the crowd tended heavily toward college age. With the University of North Carolina at Chapel Hill within a few minutes drive, it was no wonder Blue Skye was so popular.

"This place is great," Dean declared as they took their place at a table near a low, shallow stage. The girl who'd seated them collected their wine tickets. "How long's it been here? I don't remember it from when we were in college."

Leaning back in her chair, Kerry rubbed her belly. "It was here, but it wasn't Blue Skye then. It was Mother Nature's Grape."

Dean's eyebrows shot up. "That organic vineyard? Now *that* I remember. I saw the owners a couple of times at the Market."

Glancing around, Ron leaned closer. "The owners

were Sommer's parents. Stormy and Sunny Skye, remember?"

"I don't think I ever knew their names." Dean ran a hand through his hair, shoving the long bangs out of his eyes. "So when did it become Blue Skye?"

"Nineteen-ninety-eight," Kerry answered. "They decided to change the name and open up their house as a bed and breakfast."

Before Dean could ask the question foremost in his mind—*what about the haunting?*—a small, slender young man with pink-streaked blond curls approached the table carrying two glasses of pale yellow wine and a cup of juice on a tray. "Here you go," he said, flashing a wide smile. He set the wineglasses in front of Dean and Ron and handed Kerry the juice. "You folks need anything else?"

Kerry and Ron both answered in the negative. Leaning his elbows on the table, Dean grinned at the boy. "I'd like to meet the owner, actually, is he around?"

The waiter's blue eyes widened. "You want to meet Sommer?"

"Yes," Dean answered firmly. "I do."

The young man shrugged. "Well, I can ask him."

At that moment, Dean caught sight of the man himself making his way through the crowd. He seemed to be headed right for their table. "Actually, never mind," Dean said. "Here he comes now."

The young man glanced up and waved at Sommer. "Okay. I'm Cody, let me know if you need anything else."

Dean nodded, not even looking as Cody moved to the

next table. He couldn't take his eyes off the man coming toward them. When he thought about it, he wasn't even sure exactly what it was that made Sommer Skye so heart-thumpingly sexy. He was certainly an attractive man, with those huge brown eyes and the deep red hair framing a sensual, rather androgynous face. He had the type of build Dean usually preferred as well—lean, slim and athletic, his muscles streamlined rather than bulky. But those physical traits were not the reason the sight of the man made his mouth go dry and his palms sweat. No, it was something less tangible. *Something about the way he moves, or the look in his eyes*, Dean mused, taking a sip of his wine.

Sommer stopped at every table as he made his way toward where Dean, Ron and Kerry sat. He seemed to know practically everyone, and he had a smile and a friendly word for all of them. Dean found himself fascinated by the way the right side of Sommer's mouth would rise first, making his smile adorably lopsided. The way the man looked every person right in the eye, holding their gaze as if each one of them was the only person on the planet, piqued Dean's curiosity. It was very different from how he'd behaved at The Open Eye, and Dean wondered why the turnaround.

Finally, Sommer moved away from the elderly couple he'd been talking to and sauntered up to Ron, Kerry and Dean's table. "Hi," he said, flashing that impossibly sweet smile. "Glad y'all could come tonight."

"Me too. We love Karaoke Night." Ron gestured toward Dean. "Sommer, I'd like you to meet an old friend, Dean

Delapore. He went to college here with Kerry and me."

Sommer's cheeks pinked as he turned and held out a hand to Dean. "Nice to meet you, Dean. I'm Sommer Skye. Yes, it's my real name."

"Good to meet you too, Sommer." Dean shook Sommer's hand, fighting the urge to pounce on him and cuddle him like a kitten. The man's blush and the sudden shyness in those big, pretty eyes did all kinds of interesting things to Dean's insides. "I like your name. It's cool."

Sommer laughed and shrugged, retrieving his hand and coiling the fingers nervously in his hair. "I don't think anybody's ever said that before."

Leaning forward in his seat, Dean gave Sommer his very best seductive smile. "Excellent. That means you'll remember me."

Sommer's blush deepened, and Kerry snorted. "He's flirting with you, Sommer. Just tell him to quit."

Dean glared at her. She raised her eyebrows at him.

"It's okay," Sommer said, his voice soft but clearly flattered. "I don't mind."

Sticking his tongue out at Kerry and ignoring Ron's resulting laugh, Dean turned his attention back to Sommer. "So, Sommer. Kerry tells me you have a haunted house. Is that right?"

Sommer's smile faded, his expression turning cautious. "Yes, it is."

Dean frowned. Obviously, he'd hit a nerve. "I'm sorry." He laid a hand on Sommer's arm. "You don't have to tell

27

me about it if you'd rather not. It's just that I work for a paranormal investigations agency, so hauntings of all types fascinate me. You can tell me to shut up any time, it won't hurt my feelings any."

Sommer pinned Dean with a searching look, teeth capturing his lower lip in a way that threatened to make Dean lose his concentration. "Actually, Dean, I'd kind of like to talk to you about the house, if you have time."

Yes! He is so fucking me tonight! Forcing back the whoop of triumph which wanted to come out, Dean nodded. "Sure, that would be great." He turned to Kerry and Ron with a question in his eyes. "Guys?"

Kerry sighed. "Okay, okay. Just don't stay out too late."

Ron snickered. "Don't pay any attention to her, she's just practicing her mama skills."

Kerry elbowed him in the ribs, and Dean laughed. "Maybe Sommer and I can sneak off for a few minutes after karaoke. I can always come back later if you want to talk more, Sommer."

"Yeah. Or I..." Sommer's gaze dropped to the floor, veiling his eyes behind long, dark lashes. "I could drive you back to their place. After we...um, talk."

Ron and Kerry gave Dean identical knowing looks. He ignored them. "Sommer, that would be fabulous. Thank you."

Sommer looked up, his gaze meeting Dean's. The spark in his eyes made Dean's heart thump. "My pleasure. I'm looking forward to talking to you." He turned to smile at Ron and Kerry. "See y'all later."

Dean licked his lips as Sommer pivoted and walked away. The way that firm little ass moved in the snug jeans enthralled him.

Something bounced off Dean's forehead and onto the table. He blinked at Kerry, who'd thrown a rolled-up bit of paper napkin at him. "What?"

She shook her head, amusement written all over her face. "Do *not* try to get Sommer into bed tonight. It won't work."

Dean crossed his arms. "Bet it will."

"No way, man," Ron chimed in. "Sommer's great at working the crowd here, but he is seriously shy one-on-one."

Kerry nodded. "Especially with people he doesn't know."

"*Especially* especially with people he doesn't know but wants to get between the sheets," Ron added.

Kerry glared at her husband. "You're not helping."

Laughing, Dean leaned back in his chair and took a sip of his wine. "Don't yell at Ron. I already knew Mr. Skye wanted to fuck me."

Kerry sighed and shook her head as Dean and Ron both snickered. "Whatever. Just don't spend the rest of the visit moping if he turns you down."

"He won't." Shoving away the part of him which felt cold at the thought of another one-night stand, Dean flashed his most brilliant smile. "Now who's gonna sing some Elvis with me?"

♥

Kerry and Ron left two hours later, leaving Dean with hugs and, in Kerry's case, stern warnings not to try to sweet talk Sommer into sex if he was reluctant. Ron rolled his eyes behind Kerry's back as they started across the room, and Dean bit back a laugh. Sommer wanted him. The heat in the man's eyes when he looked at Dean made that clear beyond a doubt. Even Ron saw it. Kerry, usually much more observant about such things, couldn't possibly have missed it. Maybe, Dean mused, she felt protective of Sommer because of his obvious shyness.

It was a feeling Dean thought he could understand. Something about Sommer made Dean want to shield him from all the hurtful things in the world.

From his spot at the table, Dean saw Sommer stop and speak to his friends at the door. Turning around, Kerry waved over her shoulder at Dean, then left the barn hand in hand with Ron. Dean picked up the glass of zinfandel he'd bought and took a long swallow as Sommer weaved around the emptying tables toward him.

"Hi, Dean," Sommer said, leaning a hand on the chair beside Dean's. "Walk up to the house with me? I'll tell you about my ghosts, and I can show you around if you want."

Dean grinned at the nervous quaver in Sommer's voice. *Oh yeah. I'm getting laid.* "That would be awesome.

Let's go."

Pushing his chair back, Dean stood and trailed Sommer toward a small door behind the bar in the back. He was close enough to smell the man's musky cologne, underlaid with a hint of sweat. Dean breathed deep, trying not to be too obvious.

They rounded the bar and slipped through the back door into the night. Hunching his shoulders against the cold, Dean gazed around the grounds. A wide, neatly trimmed lawn stretched from the barn to the vineyard. The bare vines rasped together in the light wind. Overhead, the waxing moon shed a soft silver glow over the scene. Dean found it unbearably romantic.

Moving closer to Sommer, Dean gave him his friendliest smile. "So tell me about your ghosts."

Sommer shot him a shy sidelong grin which made him want to rip the man's clothes off and throw him down on the manicured grass. "What would you like to know?"

"What exactly you've experienced, where and when, and for how long." Dean accidentally-on-purpose brushed Sommer's arm with his, savoring the resulting hitch in Sommer's breath. "Anything you can think of, really. Every detail can help determine what sort of haunting it is, and what if anything can be done about it."

Sommer nodded, a thoughtful expression on his face. "That makes sense."

"So tell me all about it."

Sommer glanced at him again, a mixture of curiosity and fear in his eyes, but didn't say anything. Dean waited, content just to walk together through the moonlit night. A light, chilly breeze rustled through the bare branches of the trees clustered behind the house, bringing with it the sounds of music and laughter from the barn, and the lingering smell of sun-warmed grass. Finally, as they approached the wide, shallow steps leading to the front porch of the Inn, Sommer stopped and turned to Dean with a determined expression.

"I see a mist forming," he said, his voice low and quiet. "It rises from the floor in the kitchen, hovers there for a minute, then floats out the back door. It doesn't make a sound, or interact with me in any way. But I..." He drew a deep breath, his gaze skittering away to rest on the huge wooden swing swaying from the branch of a large oak in front of the house. "I can *feel* it watching me. Like it expects me to do something, but I don't know what."

Intrigued, Dean leaned against the steps' railing and regarded Sommer with keen interest. "Has anyone else seen this?"

Sommer nodded without looking at Dean. "Yeah. The cook, Lisa, saw it once, when I was in the kitchen with her."

"Is she the only one?"

"So far, yes."

"So far?"

"I've only had the Inn for four years, since my parents..." Sommer stared at the ground. "Well, they went missing. No clues to where they'd gone, or what might've happened to them. They just vanished." Raising his head again, Sommer met Dean's gaze with a surprisingly strong defiance in his own. "I'm an only child, there was no one else to look after this place, so I quit my job in Oregon and moved to Chapel Hill to take over the business. I've been seeing the mist ever since I first moved in, and no one's seen it except when they've been with me."

Moved by something he didn't quite understand, Dean reached out and laid a hand on Sommer's shoulder. "How often do you see this mist?" he asked, keeping his tone calm.

"A couple of times a week, usually."

Dean pursed his lips, thinking hard. "Did you live here, in this house, before you lived in Oregon?"

Sommer shook his head. "No. In fact, my parents were—*are*—from Portland. They moved here when I was fifteen. I didn't want to leave home, so they let me stay with my Aunt Katherine. I'd never been here until Mom and Dad turned up missing."

"Hm." Pushing away from the railing, Dean slid his hand down Sommer's arm, making sure to brush their fingers together before drawing away. "Hey, can we go inside? It's getting cold out here, and I'd love to see the kitchen, if that's okay."

Sommer's face brightened into one of those sweet, crooked smiles which made Dean's stomach flutter like he'd swallowed a flock of small birds. "That would be great. I have a few guests coming in tomorrow, but the place is empty tonight. We'll have it to ourselves. I can show you everything."

The implications in Sommer's words were not lost on Dean. He took Sommer's arm and smiled up at him, letting his lust shine on his face. "I like that idea."

Sommer's eyelids fluttered downward, hiding his eyes. His blush was clearly visible in the bright moonlight. He opened his mouth as if to speak, then closed it again and shook his head. His gaze darted up again, meeting Dean's, and Dean caught his breath at the fire in the man's eyes. Before Dean could say a word, Sommer's hand clamped onto the back of his neck and pulled him into a rough, demanding kiss.

Chapter Three

For a split second, sheer surprise held Dean immobile. He knew Sommer wanted him, and he was confident they'd end up in bed before the night was out, but he'd expected to take the initiative himself. He never would have guessed Sommer would be this aggressive.

The thoughts fleeted through Dean's brain in the space of a heartbeat, then Sommer's tongue darted into his mouth and anything resembling rational thought went right out the window. With a low moan, Dean clutched Sommer close and tilted his head to deepen the kiss.

One long, graceful hand slid down to cup Dean's ass through his snug jeans, the ones he'd worn specifically because they displayed his backside to best advantage. Dean returned the favor, grabbing a double handful of well-toned rear end and squeezing as Sommer attempted to suck his tongue out. Sommer groaned, the hand on Dean's neck moving up to fist into his hair.

Dean whimpered when Sommer's knee pushed between his legs. He rubbed himself shamelessly against the firm thigh.

"Let's go inside," Dean breathed the second Sommer

broke the kiss to bite at the juncture of neck and shoulder. "God, if you fuck as good as you kiss it'll probably kill me but I don't care."

Sommer's chuckle vibrated against Dean's throat. "No one's ever complained. Not that I'm in the habit of taking men I just met to bed."

"Mmm," Dean hummed, arching his neck for Sommer's nibbles and kisses. "I'd ask you why you're taking *me* to bed, but I don't care just as long as you fuck me through the mattress."

To Dean's relief, Sommer didn't seem inclined to answer the question Dean had half-asked. Pulling out of Dean's arms, Sommer grabbed his hand and started dragging him up the steps to the porch. "Come on. There's lube and condoms in my bedroom."

Dean's insides clenched. *Oh, my. I think I like him bossy.* Grinning, he let himself be led inside.

The front door was barely shut behind them when Sommer slammed Dean against the wall for another invasive kiss. Dean moaned, tremors running through his body at the feel of Sommer's hands sliding up under his shirt. As far as Dean was concerned, there was nothing better than a forceful man. He never would've pegged Sommer Skye for one of those men, but he wasn't about to complain. The contrast between Sommer's shy, polite public self and the man currently eating at Dean's mouth was exciting as hell.

God, I hope he's this take-charge in bed. Dean shoved a hand down the back of Sommer's jeans, fingertip just dipping into the crease of his ass. Sommer growled and shoved his tongue deep into Dean's mouth, and Dean mentally congratulated himself. Showing a bit of aggressiveness of his own, he'd found, usually brought out the animal in his bed partners. The male ones, anyhow. The women loved it when he went all Alpha on them, but in those cases he was forced to keep on playing the dominant role. He much preferred making himself submissive. Especially to a man like Sommer, whose dominant tendencies evidently only came out in the bedroom.

Bedroom. We should be in the bedroom right now. "Bedroom," Dean mumbled, the word slurred by kisses. "Where?"

Sommer waved a hand toward a half-open door to Dean's left. "There." Seemingly in no hurry to move, Sommer tilted Dean's head back by the hair and ran a smooth wet tongue up his throat.

"Oh God," Dean breathed, hanging onto Sommer's shoulders to keep from collapsing in a heap on the floor. "Can...can we go in there? You're making my legs not work."

He felt Sommer's lips curl into a smile. "Good."

Sommer's hand crept between Dean's thighs, cupping his crotch, and he whimpered. "*Please.*"

Laughing, Sommer drew away, letting a hand slide down to clasp Dean's. "I like how you beg."

"I like how you make me *want* to beg." Dean slipped an arm around Sommer's waist and hung on to one of the belt loops on the black jeans. His legs felt like rubber bands, making it difficult to walk. "I've been wanting to spread my legs for you ever since you walked into The Open Eye this afternoon."

Shoving the bedroom door open, Sommer dragged Dean inside and kicked the door shut again. "Are you always this easy?"

In spite of Sommer's teasing smile and the twinkle in his eye which made it clear he wasn't serious, a cold, ugly feeling curled in Dean's belly. He didn't know whether to label it shame, or simple loneliness. Both tended to thrive on years of one-night stands, of scorching but ultimately unfulfilling sex.

Either way, he didn't like this black, empty ache which overtook him from time to time. Strangely, no-strings sex provided both the cause and the cure. He'd learned that lesson long ago, and he intended to apply it now.

Plastering on the smile which turned men and women alike into putty, he took both of Sommer's hands and pulled him toward the bed. "Does it matter? I'm easy now, for you. So use me."

The smolder in Sommer's eyes flared into a blaze. Without another word, he grasped the hem of Dean's shirt and pulled it up. Dean lifted his arms to let the cotton slide off. Sommer tossed the garment aside. His gaze raked down Dean's body.

Heart pounding with anticipation, Dean watched Sommer watching him. Moonlight poured through the thin crimson sheers half-drawn across the big bay window, bathing the room in shimmering red-tinged light and throwing soft shadows across Sommer's face. Furniture loomed in the periphery of Dean's vision, and from the corner of his eye he saw a closed door on the other side of the room, but he couldn't be bothered to look away from Sommer long enough to notice much else. Except the bed, of course. A four-poster, he noted with delight. He wondered if Sommer had any restraints.

Sommer moved closer, dark eyes boring into Dean's. "Please tell me you're a bottom."

A shudder ran through Dean's body. "Oh yeah," he answered, his voice sounding weak and shaky in his own ears. "I'll top if I have to, but I'd rather get fucked than do the fucking."

"Good. Because I don't bottom." Sommer's mouth quirked into a wry half-smile. "Can't relax enough for it not to hurt."

Dean wasn't sure what he was supposed to say to that, so he said nothing. Instead, he undid the buttons of Sommer's shirt. He spread the fabric so he could caress the bared skin. Coarse, dark hairs rasped against his palms and the pads of his fingers, drawing a soft moan from him. Finding one hard little nipple, Dean gave it a gentle pinch.

"Oh fuck," Sommer gasped, his back arching. One hand clamped onto Dean's shoulder, the other grasping him by the hair. "Bite it."

Heat shot through Dean's groin. He yanked the shirt

down, forcing Sommer to let go of him long enough for the garment to slide down his arms to the floor. Letting Sommer push his head downward, he dug his teeth into the nipple he'd just pinched and gave it a tug. Sommer groaned, his fist tightening in Dean's hair. Picking up Sommer's cues, Dean bit harder, sucking and pulling. Sommer cursed and trembled and clutched at Dean's hair hard enough to hurt. Humming his approval, Dean drew back to lick the bit of abused skin before switching his mouth to the other nipple. Sommer tasted clean and faintly salty with the sweat of desire, and Dean wanted to lap it all up.

He was so caught up in the feel of flesh bruising between his teeth, Sommer had to literally push him away. Sommer's nipple came out of Dean's mouth with an audible pop, and Sommer hissed. Dean straightened up, his gaze meeting Sommer's. The intense desire there made him quiver inside.

"Take off the rest of your clothes," Sommer ordered in a voice husky with lust. "Then lie down on the bed, on your back."

Dean hurried to obey. He toed off his sneakers, undid his jeans and wriggled them down to his knees. Plopping onto the edge of the bed, he pulled his pants and socks off in a tangle of fabric. He hadn't worn underwear, as he'd hoped for an encounter of the hot sex kind with Sommer. Judging by the look in Sommer's eyes, it had been a good move.

Naked, Dean slid to the middle of the king-sized mattress and lay back, arms stretched languidly above his head, and gave Sommer a sultry smile. "What do you want, Sommer?"

Sommer licked his lips. "Spread your legs."

Dean did as he was told, opening his thighs wide. He loved the way Sommer stared at him, like his body was a ripe, juicy fruit unexpectedly appearing before a man starving in a desert. His pulse raced, and he could smell the musk of his own lust. The part of his brain still functioning wished Sommer would stop devouring him with his eyes and start using that gorgeous mouth instead.

Holding Sommer's gaze, Dean cupped his balls in one hand and grasped his stiff shaft with the other. "You want to watch me jerk off?"

Sommer blinked and started, as if coming out of a trance. "No. I just wanted to look at you for a minute."

"Well, the way you're looking at me is about to make me come." Wetting the pad of one thumb in his mouth, Dean pressed it to the tip of his cock. He rubbed slow, tight circles against the tiny opening, sending electric shocks through his body. A rough moan tore from his throat. "C'mon, get over here."

Dean hadn't finished speaking before Sommer was suddenly there, batting his hands away and nuzzling between his legs. The speed with which the man moved was shocking. Soft lips closed over the head of Dean's prick, slick tongue penetrating the slit, and he let out a sharp cry. His hands dug into Sommer's hair. The strands felt cool and silky between his fingers. Sommer hummed and sucked Dean's cock deep into his throat.

The squeal that emerged from Dean was far from dignified, but he didn't care. Right then, nothing existed apart from Sommer's warm, wet mouth on his cock, Sommer's elegant hands kneading the insides of his thighs. Moaning, Dean hooked both hands behind his knees and pulled his legs up and apart, giving Sommer more room to play.

Sommer allowed Dean's prick to slide out of his mouth, moved up and planted a moist kiss on Dean's belly. Before Dean could summon the presence of mind to protest, Sommer reached up and traced his lips with his fingertips.

"Suck my fingers," Sommer commanded, the right corner of his mouth lifting in a smile which managed to be sexy and innocent at the same time. "Get them good and wet, so I can get you ready to fuck."

As often as he bottomed, Dean no longer needed much preparation. But if Sommer wanted to finger his ass, who was he to argue? Holding Sommer's gaze, he parted his lips and let Sommer slide two fingers inside. The long, fine-boned digits tasted of something faintly spicy. Dean's questing tongue found a callous on the first knuckle of Sommer's index finger. He gave it a slow lick, enjoying the roughness against his tongue.

Once Dean had coated Sommer's fingers with saliva, Sommer pulled them out of Dean's mouth and slid them between his buttocks. "Keep yourself spread open for me," Sommer whispered, rubbing one dripping fingertip against Dean's hole. "You're beautiful like this."

It wasn't the first time Dean had heard those words, or similar ones. He was a very attractive man, and he knew it. Lots of men and women had told him so. It was nice to hear, of course, but nothing new for him. Yet for reasons he couldn't pinpoint, hearing Sommer call him beautiful sent his spirit soaring. Maybe because for the first time, the compliment seemed not only sincere, but without expectation. Something told him Sommer wouldn't expect anything more from him than he was willing to give, unlike many lovers Dean had been with over the years.

Not that he could currently think of anything he didn't want to give Sommer.

The feel of a finger pressing inside him shattered Dean's half-formed musings. "Oooooh, oh God," he groaned, hips canting upward. "More."

Sommer obliged by pushing another finger into Dean's ass. He leaned down and bit the place where the tendon on the inside of Dean's thigh strained tight. Dean yelped. He twisted his head enough to see Sommer's face. Sommer gave him a sinful smile, and licked the spot he'd just bitten. The bright moonlight revealed two dark semicircles glistening with saliva on Dean's skin. *That's gonna bruise.* He grinned, already picturing the purple marks he'd have the next day.

Inside him, Sommer's fingers crooked to brush the sweet spot. Dean let out a wail. "God, fuck me!"

Sommer rubbed his cheek against Dean's calf and twisted his fingers in Dean's hole, drawing another sharp cry from him. "You're awfully impatient," Sommer observed. He wrapped his free hand around Dean's cock and squeezed. "I'd rather not rush, if that's okay with you."

With a mighty effort, Dean managed to get out several nearly coherent sentences. "I can get it up again, just... Come, gotta... Too hot, you're... What you're doing... I, I can't, I need... Fuck, just fucking get me off!"

To Dean's supreme annoyance, Sommer laughed. *Not fair!* Dean's pride screamed. *He shouldn't get to be all sweet and nice and last longer than me. Fuck. Fuck, fuck, fuck.*

"Put your hands above your head," Sommer ordered, that ridiculously sweet smile lighting his face and forming a stark contrast to what he was saying. "Keep your legs spread."

In an instant, lust and need blew annoyance out of the water. Dean did as he was told.

Sommer's gaze skimmed Dean's body, the motion slow and deliberate. Dean could practically feel the heat in Sommer's eyes, like a flame licking his skin. When Sommer's gaze met his, Dean felt truly naked for the first time in longer than he could remember. Naked and vulnerable. Spread like a feast, or a sacrifice. Lying there with legs splayed obscenely wide, cock hard and leaking, his soon-to-be lover kneeling mostly clothed between his legs with two fingers in his ass and a hand stroking his prick, Dean felt like Sommer's sex toy. A plaything, something to be used as needed and ignored the rest of the time.

The kinkier parts of him loved that feeling. But the look in Sommer's eyes said that to him, at least, Dean was no toy. Even if this ended up being just another one-night stand, Sommer clearly saw him as something more than a willing hole.

That scared him. Not least because it drew out the tiny spark of hope that *this* time it could be something more than a meaningless fuck. That hope lingered beneath the surface of every anonymous sexual encounter in every motel or apartment or club back room, just waiting for the right person to make it flare to life.

Dean didn't want to think about that. Not now, with Sommer's probing fingers and tugging hand bringing him closer and closer to the brink.

Turning away from the oddly tender light in Sommer's eyes, Dean dug his fingers into the bedclothes. "God, yes. Close."

"Mmmm," Sommer purred, the sound like a physical touch. "Good. I want to see you shoot all over yourself." Bending, he flicked his tongue over the head of Dean's cock. "I want to feel your asshole grab my fingers when you come."

"Fuck," Dean swore, and came so hard his back bowed off the mattress.

He lay there, twitching in the aftermath of orgasm, and stared at the ceiling. It was the old-fashioned wooden kind, the sort you found in early 1900s Victorian houses. There was a name for it, he knew, but he couldn't remember it. Between his legs, Sommer was busy daubing his fingers in the semen puddled on Dean's stomach. The fingers of his other hand remained buried in Dean's ass, sliding and twisting, curling every few seconds to nail his prostate.

Dean kept his gaze fixed on the ceiling and let Sommer play with him. If he looked into Sommer's eyes, the longing for something more than a great fuck might take him over. He wasn't ready for that.

A slick, wet tongue dug into the bend of his hip, and he drew a sharp breath. A cool dry scent like old books and dust wound through the stronger smells of sweat, come and desire. Something about it, the normalcy of it in the midst of sex, made his heart ache.

The mattress shifted, the pressure vanishing from Dean's ass, and Sommer's face appeared above him. "Dean? Are you okay?"

Apprehension and uncertainty radiated from Sommer, and Dean felt a twinge of guilt. *It's not his fault I'm all fucked up and scared of relationships. He probably doesn't want one anyway. We're just fucking, that's all. Stop trying to make it something it's not.*

Summoning a smile, Dean cupped Sommer's face in his hands and drew him down for a gentle kiss. "I'm fine. But I think you shorted out my brain."

Relief echoed in Sommer's laugh. "You said you could get hard again. I hope you can, because I'm going to want you to come again when I fuck you."

A delicious shiver ran up Dean's spine. "Damn, I love how bossy you get in bed. That's so hot."

"You like that, huh?"

"Mm-hm."

"You get off on being ordered around?"

"Only during sex. Try it any other time, you probably wouldn't like the result. Just ask my boss." Dean nipped Sommer's bottom lip, then licked away the sting. "But when it comes to fucking? Hell yeah. I love being told what to do."

The teasing sparkle faded from Sommer's eyes, and a dark hunger slid in to replace it. Dean stilled, waiting for whatever Sommer would say next. His cock twitched in anticipation.

To his disappointment, Sommer pushed up on his hands, scooted backward off the bed and stood up. "I'm going to finish undressing, then get the condoms and lube," he explained before Dean could say anything.

Dean let his eyelids droop to half-mast. "And what do I do while you get naked and grab the goods?"

Leaning over, Sommer brushed a kiss across Dean's knee. "Rub that come all over yourself. Eat some of it. I think that would be hot."

"Yeah." Dean scooped up a bit of spunk with one finger. He stuck the finger in his mouth and sucked off the thick, bitter liquid, enjoying the way Sommer's eyes hazed over at the sight. "Mmmm. Good."

Sommer's lips parted, but he didn't say anything. Dean was glad. If Sommer wanted to taste his come, he really didn't want to know. They were never going to get to that stage, so there was no point in thinking about it.

Sliding his hand into the rapidly drying semen splattered on his belly, Dean coated his fingers and brought them to his mouth. He licked each finger clean one by one.

Sommer groaned, his gaze darting back and forth between the drawer he was digging through and Dean's display. "God, you're hot." He threw a condom and a bottle of liquid lube on the bed and reached down to pull his shoes off.

"Pot. Kettle," Dean said, watching Sommer skin out of his jeans and underwear. Sommer's cock sprang free and hit his belly with a damp smack. He was uncut, the foreskin pulled back so that the head glistened in the moonlight. Dean's mouth watered. "Damn. I can't wait to get *that* in me."

The corner of Sommer's mouth tugged up, making Dean's chest tight. How could he already be addicted to the man's smile?

"Good, because I can't wait anymore." Sommer climbed onto the bed, stalking Dean on hands and knees like a cat. His skin seemed to glow, the light shimmering over lean muscles as they shifted with his movement. His hair fell forward to shadow his face. Between his legs, his erect cock hung in silhouette. A pearl of pre-come gathered at the tip and dripped in slow motion, connected to its point of origin by a shining liquid thread which thinned and broke as Dean watched.

Dean thought he'd never seen anything so alluring. Following a sudden whim, he stretched out a hand toward Sommer. "Come kiss me."

Sommer straddled his hips, leaned down and pressed a tender kiss to his lips. A lock of Sommer's hair tickled Dean's cheek. The sleek strands smelled of apple-scented shampoo, enhancing rather than masking the scents of spunk and male arousal. Dean opened his mouth with a sigh and let Sommer's tongue in to wind around his. The fronts of Sommer's knees pressed against the backs of Dean's spread thighs, the hairs rough and scratchy on his skin.

Dean ran both hands up and down Sommer's sides as the kiss grew heated. His skin was warm and smooth beneath Dean's palms.

"How do you want it?" Sommer murmured, lips brushing a feathery trail down Dean's throat. "On your back, or on all fours?"

"I don't really care, as long as I get your cock up my ass pretty damn soon." Dean dug his fingers into Sommer's back and arched his neck, the feel of Sommer's lips and tongue sending shockwaves through him. "I'll do whatever you want."

Privately, he hoped Sommer preferred him on hands and knees, so he wouldn't have to see whatever there was to see in Sommer's eyes. But not if it would keep Sommer from fucking him.

Sommer drew back and laid a warm palm on Dean's cheek. "I want you on your back. So I can see your face. Is that okay?"

Dean bit his lip. "Sure," he heard himself say.

Sommer's smile made the small lie worthwhile.

Resuming his previous position kneeling between Dean's legs, Sommer snatched up the condom packet and tore it open. "Lift your legs up. Let me see your hole."

Dean obediently bent his knees to his chest, hands around the backs of his thighs to hold the position. He watched Sommer roll the condom over his cock. The man had such graceful hands. Dean thought he could spend hours just watching Sommer's long, slim fingers move.

A soft chuckle made Dean look up. Sommer smiled down at him, one hand around the base of his cock and the other warm on Dean's thigh. "What are you thinking about, Dean?"

"Your hands," Dean answered, his brain too blood-deprived to bother with anything but the truth. "They're sexy."

Sommer's head tilted, one shoulder lifting in a semi-shrug. His embarrassment at the compliment was palpable. It was adorable, and just made Dean want him more.

Picking up the bottle of lube, Sommer poured a generous handful and coated his latex-sheathed cock. He leaned forward, resting his weight on one hand and pressing two slick fingers of the other into Dean's ass.

"Are you ready?" Sommer whispered, staring into Dean's eyes.

Mouth dry and heart racing, Dean nodded. Sommer pulled his fingers out of Dean and rested the tip of his prick against the stretched hole. His hips rocked forward, pushing the head of his cock inside, and Dean gasped.

"Oh fuck yes."

Sommer didn't speak, but the rough rasp of his breathing announced his excitement loud and clear. Another sharp thrust, and his shaft was fully buried in Dean's body. Dean shut his eyes and concentrated on the pleasurable burn in his hole and the fullness in his ass. Now if only Sommer would move, drag that thick cock over his prostate a few times...

A slide out, a thrust in, and Dean's wish came true. He cried out as Sommer's prick nailed his gland over and over. "God, yes. Harder."

Sommer raised up long enough to wrap Dean's legs around his waist. He fell forward onto both hands, staring down at Dean with fire in his eyes. "You want me to fuck you hard, huh?"

"Oh yeah," Dean answered, feeling weak and breathless. His cock was fully hard again and dripping pre-come on his belly. "Pound my ass good."

Dean had been with a lot of men in his life. Most of them, he'd found, either held back for fear of hurting him, or fucked him brutally hard without regard to his comfort or pleasure. Sommer did neither. His movements were perfect, thrusting hard enough to rattle Dean's bones and send electricity arcing through his body from his gland, but with enough control that Dean knew he wouldn't be hurting later.

He felt like Goldilocks, having sampled far too many men who were Too Little or Too Much in bed and finally finding one who was Just Right. The thought was so strange, it drew a strangled laugh from him.

"Something funny?" Sommer panted, not breaking his rhythm for a second.

Shaking his head, Dean reached up to caress the strong, lean arms keeping Sommer's full weight off him. "Just really liking where I am right now. Underneath you, with your cock up my ass."

"Good. I like it too." Sommer gave a particularly hard thrust, causing a drop of sweat to roll off his chin and onto Dean's face. He bent and licked it off. "Fuck, you feel good. Gonna come soon."

Dean wanted to tell Sommer how close he was, how amazing it felt having Sommer fuck him, but the sudden swelling of Sommer's shaft inside him robbed him of speech. Moaning, he buried both hands in Sommer's hair and pulled him down into a deep, wet kiss.

Sommer growled. His thrusts lost their rhythm, his hips pistoning in short, sharp strokes which zinged over Dean's gland and made him tremble all over. Dean let out a keening wail as orgasm washed over him, the sound muffled by Sommer's mouth on his. His semen spread warm and slick over his belly just as Sommer jerked and gasped into the kiss. Dean felt Sommer's cock pulse as he came.

In a brief blaze of semi-coherence, Dean wondered what it meant that they'd come at the same time, or if it meant anything at all. He'd never come at the exact same time as a lover before. It was good—wonderful, in fact— but the fact that it had happened with a stranger made him uncomfortable. It ought to be something special, an experience to share with someone he loved rather than a one-night stand.

Take what you can get, he admonished himself, stroking Sommer's hair as the kiss turned slow and languid. *No way you'll ever have another relationship longer than a few months, and you'll sure as hell never find someone else to love, so be grateful for the good stuff when you get it.*

Eventually, Sommer broke the kiss and gave Dean a wide, bright smile. "Wow."

Laughing, Dean tucked a hank of sweat-damp hair behind Sommer's ear. "You said it."

Drawing his softening cock carefully from Dean's hole, Sommer took the condom off and dropped it over the side of the bed onto the floor. He flopped onto his back, one arm stretched out toward Dean. "Come here."

Dean's sense of emotional self-preservation warned him against lying in Sommer's arms in the afterglow. He didn't cuddle with his casual fucks, and he couldn't afford to start thinking of Sommer as anything more than that. But the man's bare chest with its sprinkling of dark hair made a tempting pillow, and he saw nothing in those brown eyes but the simple desire to hold him.

Such honesty was rare in Dean's experience, and he found it irresistible. Rolling over, he molded his body to Sommer's and let his head rest on Sommer's chest. He slid an arm around Sommer's waist and slung a leg over his thigh. Sommer's arms went around him, and a kiss was pressed to the top of his head. He sighed, his body relaxing in Sommer's embrace. He felt warm, safe and content.

Maybe, he thought as his eyes drifted closed, he could handle this post-sex snuggling thing after all.

Chapter Four

In his dream, Dean heard drums. The rhythmic thumping wound through his subconscious, nudging him ever-so-gently toward wakefulness. As frequently happened when he dreamed, he was fully aware of being asleep, his dream cradling him in warm, living darkness like being back in the womb. It was strangely comforting, and he didn't want to leave it just yet. But the thumping was growing louder by the second, too irregular for a heartbeat and too insistent to be ignored.

"Sommer! Open this fucking door *right now*, dammit!"

It was Kerry's voice, and she sounded furious. Dean's eyes flew open. Sunlight poured through the window in a golden flood, bringing out the deep burgundy of Sommer's bedspread and the rich hues of the bed's wooden posts. Dean had a split second to process the cream-colored walls and the huge antique wardrobe which almost brushed the high ceiling before realization hit him.

It was morning. He'd fallen asleep in Sommer's arms, and there he'd stayed all night.

He sat up just in time to meet Sommer's startled, sleep-addled gaze. Sommer's dark eyes went wide as he evidently realized the same thing Dean did. "Oh no. We fell asleep."

"Yeah. And Kerry sounds like killing us both right now." Dean hopped off the bed, found his jeans and started pulling them on. "You go first."

Sommer rose and stretched, looking not at all anxious to face Kerry's wrath. "Why don't you go? You've known her longer."

"Yeah, but she'll hurt me. You, she likes." Dean bit his lip, torn between Kerry's increasingly frantic shouts and the mouthwatering display of Sommer's nude body gleaming in the morning sun. The way the lean muscles shifted as he moved made Dean's palms itch to touch him. "You know, Sommer, if you don't put some clothes on I'll be forced to molest you right here and now, and then it'll be Death By Pregnant Woman for both of us."

Sommer laughed, the sound husky with sleep and unbearably sexy. He swayed toward Dean, mouth hitching into that crooked little smile. "Guess I'd better get dressed then. It'd be pretty embarrassing for us big tough he-men to be torn apart by a five-foot-nothing pregnant girl."

Shaking his head, Dean let himself be swept into Sommer's arms and pulled snug against his warm naked body. "You're gonna get us in trouble."

"No, I won't." Sommer rubbed the tip of his nose against Dean's. "One kiss, and I'll go smooth her feathers."

Dean knew he shouldn't. Bad enough that he'd accidentally—it *was* an accident, wasn't it?—fallen asleep and spent the entire night in Sommer's bed. Indulging in morning-after kisses and nuzzles just made it harder to say "so long" and never look back when he had to leave. But he found himself unable to resist Sommer's sweet smile and sparkling eyes. Winding his arms around Sommer's neck, Dean tilted his head and parted his lips for Sommer's kiss.

The sound of the front door opening startled them apart. Kerry's angry voice and Ron's calmer one sounded from the foyer.

"Oh crap," Sommer muttered. "I forgot they had a key."

"A key? Why?"

"For emergencies." Sommer winced when the pounding resumed, on his bedroom door this time. "Dammit. I'd better get dressed."

Dean ran to the bedroom door while Sommer snatched his jeans off the floor and yanked them on. He had the zipper up and was fastening the button when Kerry started talking again.

"Dean, you better be in there," Kerry growled. "'Cause I am going to *kill* you."

"Way to make a guy let you in, Kerry," Dean called through the closed door.

"See, I told you he was fine," Ron proclaimed, calm as ever. "They were just—"

"I know!" The doorknob rattled. "Are y'all coming out here or not?"

Relief cut a wide swath through the righteous fury in

Kerry's voice, and Dean felt terrible for having made her worry. He glanced behind him and raised his eyebrows at Sommer, silently asking permission. Sommer gave the door an apprehensive look, but nodded anyway.

Dean opened the door and peered cautiously from around its protective wooden bulk. "Hey, Kerry. Sorry I didn't call or anything. We kind of fell asleep."

She smacked his bare shoulder hard, but her blue eyes were smiling. "You fucker, you scared me to death."

"Sorry," he repeated, and meant it. He frowned, taking in her flushed cheeks. "Are you okay? You want to sit down?"

"Why don't we all go in the kitchen?" Sommer suggested, walking up to the door. "I'll make us some breakfast."

Ron sidled up behind his wife, wrapped his arms around her shoulders and kissed the top of her head. "Sounds good to me. I'm starved." He dropped a hand down to caress Kerry's swollen belly. "Junior and his mama could probably use some breakfast too, especially after all that unnecessary worrying."

"Yeah, I guess." Kerry leaned her head against Ron's shoulder and rested a hand over his. She shot a stern look at Dean and Sommer. "Neither of you is off the hook, you know. 'Call home' is always rule number one if you're not coming back when you're expected."

Sommer laughed, his warm bare chest pressing against Dean's back. "Have I ever told you what a wonderful mother you're going to be?"

Kerry arched an eyebrow at him. "Flattery will get you nowhere."

Dean wanted to make a smart-ass remark, but the feel of Sommer's skin against his and the lingering smell of sex conspired to dry the words in his throat. Unable to help himself, he pressed back against Sommer's body, turning his head to nuzzle the man's jaw. Sommer's arm slid around his waist, holding him close. He could feel Sommer's breath on his ear, and he bit back a moan.

Ron chuckled. "Maybe we should go away and leave you two alone."

"Oh no. We won't see either of them for a week if we do that." Kerry grasped Dean's wrist, squeezing gently. "Come on, guys. Let's have some breakfast. Sommer, do you have any guests coming today?"

"Yeah, a few." Pulling away from Dean, Sommer wandered over to the big wardrobe against the wall and swung open the door. He reached in and brought out a pale blue long-sleeved T-shirt with the University of North Carolina at Chapel Hill logo on the front. "Two sets of college parents and a woman on a solo biking tour of North Carolina, if I remember right."

"Cool. We'll help you get everything ready." Dropping Dean's wrist, Kerry stepped out of Ron's embrace, turned and kissed him on the cheek. "C'mon, honey. You and I can start breakfast while Sommer and Dean get themselves presentable."

"Hey, I'm presentable," Dean protested. He glanced down at himself, and grimaced at the crust of dried semen covering his front. "Okay, so maybe not quite."

Ron chuckled. "Must've been some night."

Sommer groaned and hung his head. Dean grinned. "Oh yeah. It was."

Sighing, Kerry grabbed Ron's wrist and dragged him toward the kitchen. "Get cleaned up and get on out here," she called over her shoulder. "And no fucking in the shower."

Kerry's footsteps echoed across the hardwood floor to the back of the house, followed by Ron's snickering. Dean shook his head, a smile tugging at his lips. He was glad Kerry had evidently forgiven him for not calling. He loved his friends, and certainly hadn't meant to worry them.

Turning around, he glanced at Sommer, who sat on the edge of the bed pulling on a pair of blue and white running shoes. "Sorry about that. Kerry can be kind of overwhelming sometimes."

"So I see. I've known her and Ron for a couple of years now, but I've never had her mad at me until now." Sommer knotted the last lace and stood up. "You're welcome to use my shower if you want. The bathroom's right through there." He gestured to the door on the other side of the room.

Dean studied Sommer's face. Sommer smiled, and something deep inside Dean tightened painfully. He looked away. "Naw, I'll just swab off with a washcloth, if that's okay."

"Sure. I'll be in the kitchen with Kerry and Ron." Sommer crossed to the bedroom door, stopped and turned around again. "Dean?"

"Yeah?" Dean scraped at the dried spunk on his belly. His fingernail caught and pulled the matted hairs, causing bits of white to flake off.

"I'm glad you stayed."

Something in Sommer's voice made Dean look up. Sommer was watching him with an oddly serious expression. A strange mingling of warm comfort and near panic blossomed in Dean's chest. He was *so* not ready for Sommer to look at him like that. Like he was someone Sommer might consider keeping.

He forced a smile. "Yeah. Me too."

They stood there staring at each other for a long moment. Dean fought the urge to fidget under Sommer's penetrating gaze.

The smell of coffee brewing wafted from the kitchen. Sommer blinked, seeming to shake himself. "Um. Okay, I'm gonna go help cook. Take a left down the hall when you leave the bedroom, the kitchen's at the end of the hall. See you in a few minutes."

"Yeah, see you."

With a quick smile, Sommer slipped out the door and shut it behind him. Dean stumbled to the bed and dropped onto the mattress. He sat there until his trembling stopped, then went into the bathroom to clean up.

When he sauntered into the bright, airy kitchen a few minutes later, belly scrubbed clean and clothes back on, Sommer was nowhere to be seen. Kerry and Ron sat at the table, hunched over coffee, eggs and toast.

"Where's Sommer?" Dean asked, heading for the coffeepot.

"Outside, talking on the phone." Kerry waved a hand toward the cabinet to the left of the one Dean was currently peering into. "Mugs are in there. Sommer's got homemade cinnamon rolls in the oven."

"Wow, that was fast." Taking a large blue mug with white ducks painted on it from the cabinet, Dean poured himself a cup of rich-smelling coffee. "I know I didn't take *that* long cleaning up."

"He makes several batches at a time and freezes them. That way, he can just take some out of the freezer and stick 'em in the oven when he needs it." Ron shook his head as Dean spooned sugar into his coffee and topped it with a generous amount of the toffee-nut creamer sitting next to the coffeepot. "You're ruining it, man."

"Hey, if this is as strong as it smells, it needs extra fixing up to keep it from taking the lining off my esophagus." Dean took a careful sip. The dark, smoky flavor exploded on his tongue. "Oh yeah. This would totally get up and walk away if I didn't cut it with the sweet stuff."

The back door swung open and Sommer walked inside, a cell phone in his hand. He kicked the door shut and fell into a nearby chair. "Damn."

"What is it?" Kerry asked, a forkful of scrambled eggs halfway to her mouth.

"One of my reservations for tomorrow night canceled. That's the third one in the last two weeks." With a deep sigh, Sommer leaned his elbows on the table and rested his chin in his hands. "I'm losing more money all the time. If it weren't for the winery and Karaoke Night, this business would've folded months ago. I don't know what to do."

Sommer looked sad and lost, and Dean's heart went out to him. Moving to the table, Dean set his mug down and eased himself into the chair beside Sommer. "Have you thought about hiring a financial advisor?" he asked, resting a hand on Sommer's shoulder. "My boss was telling me once that he hired one when he first started up Bay City Paranormal Investigations. He said he would've been out of business within a year without her help."

Sommer's shoulders hitched in a halfhearted shrug. "I've thought about it, yeah. I'm crap at money management, so I could sure use the help. It's just..." He trailed off, dark eyes inexplicably sorrowful.

"Just what?" Dean prompted. He raked his fingers through Sommer's satin-soft hair.

"Nothing." Sommer stood and crossed the large, airy kitchen to the oven. He flipped on the oven light and peeked through the glass. "Cinnamon rolls'll be ready soon."

Sipping his coffee, Dean watched Sommer from under his eyelashes. The man seemed troubled, and something told Dean the business's financial problems weren't entirely to blame.

He bit back the urge to prod Sommer until he told Dean exactly what was bothering him. *Just because he fucked you doesn't give you the right to stick your nose in his private business. Leave it alone.*

After an awkward couple of minutes, conversation started up again. While they polished off the cinnamon rolls, Dean managed to partly satisfy his curiosity about Sommer by asking endless questions about winemaking. Sommer answered every one without complaint. His knowledge of—and obvious enthusiasm for—the craft was impressive. As he talked, the worry lines vanished from his face and his brown eyes shone with undisguised joy.

Watching Sommer's expressive features, Dean began to have an inkling of what was truly bothering him. Sommer seemed like the type of person who enjoyed the creativity and artfulness of a trade such as winemaking, but hated the day-to-day drudgery of running a business. He decided to try to talk to Sommer as soon as he could get him alone. If he was right, he'd do his damnedest to persuade Sommer to hire help for the business end so he'd have time to handle the creative end himself.

After breakfast, Ron offered to clean up while Kerry and Dean helped Sommer get ready for his guests. Dean had no clue what was involved in such preparation, but he was more than willing to help. Especially if it involved being alone in a room with Sommer.

Just to talk, he promised himself, though he knew his resolve would unravel at the slightest touch from Sommer. The slightest look, even. Just one of those lopsided smiles aimed his way, or the faintest wisp of desire in those big dark eyes, and he'd be putty in Sommer's hands.

Following Sommer and Kerry upstairs to the guestrooms, he tried to figure out what it was about Sommer that drew him so. He'd been with plenty of men who were more experienced, more skilled, better looking. Maybe not *much* better looking, true, but the fact remained he'd been with some extremely hot men before, and he'd never had trouble saying goodbye in the morning. Or, more often, immediately after sex. This time, he'd not only spent the night, he'd stayed for breakfast and even agreed to do housework. Why?

He would've liked to blame it on the prospect of witnessing the apparition Sommer had described the night before. He hadn't forgotten, and he *did* want very much to see it. But he knew that wasn't why he'd stayed. He just couldn't figure out what *was* the reason he was still here instead of back at Ron and Kerry's house.

At the top of the stairs, Sommer turned his shy smile to Dean. "Come help me set up the rooms? I'll give you the grand tour."

A bubble of warmth expanded in Dean's chest. He returned Sommer's smile, and knew it looked sappy as hell, but he couldn't make himself care. "Okay, sure."

Sommer beamed. "Great. Kerry, are you sure you're up to doing this stuff? You're more than welcome to just relax on the porch, or in the living room."

Kerry waved a dismissive hand. "Please. Pregnant does not equal disabled. I'll take care of the bathrooms, I know what to do."

Chuckling, Sommer leaned over and kissed her cheek. "Thanks. I owe you."

"You do not." Kerry walked over to a narrow door set in the pale yellow wall of the upstairs hallway. When she opened it, Dean glimpsed a deep linen closet full of neatly folded sheets and fluffy towels. Grabbing an armful of towels, she quirked an eyebrow at Sommer and Dean. "Try not to get man-goo all over the beds, okay? The parents in particular might not appreciate it."

Sommer blushed bright red. "God, Kerry. Stop it."

Unable to resist, Dean wrapped both arms around Sommer's waist. "We'll try to resist," he purred, and bit Sommer's shoulder.

Snickering, Kerry wandered down the hall and disappeared into the last doorway. Sommer shook his head, the bright pink fading from his cheeks. "She's got some mouth on her."

"Ron says the same thing, but he usually has a big grin on his face when he says it." Dean laughed at Sommer's renewed blush. Letting his arms drop, Dean gave Sommer a light smack on the ass. "Let's get busy, huh? You promised me a tour."

"So I did." Smiling, Sommer took Dean's hand in his, lacing their fingers together.

Trying to ignore how right it felt to hold Sommer's hand, Dean followed him into the first guestroom.

It took less than an hour to get the rooms ready for

the expected guests, sweep the hallway floors and clean the bathrooms. To Dean's irritation, he and Sommer were never alone for more than a minute or two at a time. Kerry kept popping in, and Ron came up to help after he finished in the kitchen.

Dean sighed as they all trooped downstairs into the kitchen. *So you didn't get to talk to him alone. Big deal. It's not like you're gonna be hanging around here. You have to go back home in a week and some change anyway.*

The reminder was not a welcome one. Shoving the uncomfortable thought away, Dean followed the others into the kitchen.

Sommer poured them all tall glasses of iced tea. Dean leaned against the counter and took a long drink, watching Sommer do the same. The way Sommer's throat worked as he swallowed had Dean shifting uncomfortably in his suddenly too-snug jeans.

Ron drained his glass and sat back in his chair with a contented sigh. "That just hit the spot. Sommer, can I come work for you? I never get breakfast and iced tea at my job."

Sommer laughed. "Be careful what you ask for, Ron. I'm a complete tech idiot, I could use some computer help around here."

His expression turning serious, Ron leaned forward and rested his forearms on the table. "What do you need, man? I'll help you if I can."

"Oh no, I couldn't ask you to do that," Sommer protested, eyes wide. "It's not that big a deal anyway, I was just having some spreadsheet trouble. I'm sure I can work it out."

"No, it's no problem at all. Why don't I give it a look, maybe I—"

"What the fuck's *that?*" Kerry shrieked, leaping from her chair and backing against the far wall.

Startled by Kerry's outburst, Dean followed her frightened gaze.

Something white and amorphous was rising from the wide, pale planks of the kitchen floor.

Chapter Five

As the four of them watched, the misty form pulled free of the wood and hovered in midair, undulating in slow motion. Through it, Dean could just make out the small panes in the back door window.

"Oh my God, that's it," Sommer whispered. He moved closer to Dean, staring wide-eyed at the thing in the middle of the room. "That's what I've been seeing."

"Is it dangerous?" Ron asked in a hushed, shaky voice. He still sat at the table, watching the filmy shape with mingled curiosity and fear.

Sommer shook his head. "I don't think so. At least, it's never hurt me before."

Dean leaned his shoulder against Sommer's. "Have you tried to communicate with it?"

The surprise in Sommer's eyes said it all. "No."

Taking his hand, Dean held Sommer's gaze. "Try it. Try talking to it."

Sommer looked terrified at the prospect, but he nodded anyway. Keeping Dean's hand firmly clutched in his, he took a tentative step closer to the thing. "Uh. Wh-

what are you? What do you want?"

No response. Dean wasn't surprised. Apparitions sometimes communicated with living people, but they didn't often respond to direct questions.

He was still trying to think of something else to try when the thing suddenly drifted toward the back door. It floated straight through the solid wood.

"It always does that," Sommer said, sounding disappointed. "I guess it doesn't want to talk to me."

Inspiration hit Dean, and he acted on it right away. "Come on." He pulled Sommer toward the door through which the thing had disappeared. "Let's follow it."

Sommer blinked, but didn't argue. "Why?"

"Maybe this is its way of communicating with you," Dean explained as he flung the door open and raced across the porch, dragging Sommer with him. "Maybe it's trying to show you something."

Sommer didn't say anything, but Dean felt his interest in the way his fingers clenched around Dean's.

Looking over his shoulder, Dean saw Kerry and Ron gaping at them from the kitchen door. "Stay there," he called. "If anything else happens, write it down."

Ron gave him a salute, then pulled a protesting Kerry back inside. Satisfied, Dean turned his attention back to the thing he and Sommer were chasing.

The nebulous shape was out in the yard now, drifting across the grass toward the woods behind the house. It was barely visible in the bright sunlight. Dean and Sommer took off after it, jogging to keep up.

The morning was already warm for January, and promised to be warmer still later on. Sweat dewed Dean's forehead by the time they reached the forest. Sommer didn't even slow down, but trailed the apparition between the trees. Dean's sneakers pounded the dry leaf mold with a dull thud as he and Sommer ran. The bare branches rasped and sighed in the light breeze.

They'd run almost a hundred yards, near as Dean could figure, when the shape stopped moving, hovered for a second, then suddenly vanished. Sommer skidded to a halt, staring around with a wild look in his eyes. "Where'd it go?"

"Disappeared." Dean walked over to the spot where the apparition had stopped, in a small clearing floored with grass and weeds. "Huh. Well, it was worth a shot."

Sommer's face fell. "Damn. I was really hoping we might find something."

"You still might. Just because this time didn't pan out, doesn't mean you can't keep trying."

"I guess." Disappointment filled Sommer's voice. He stuck his hands in his back pockets and stared morosely at the spot where the apparition had disappeared.

Tilting his head, Dean took a good, long look at the man he'd spent a night and most of a morning with. Sommer's hair gleamed a hundred shades of red in the dappled sunshine. Perspiration made his golden-brown skin glow. The sun shone through his long lashes to cast soft shadows on his cheeks. His well-worn jeans did nothing to hide the sleek contours of hip, leg and ass.

Dean wondered what it would feel like to fuck on a forest floor.

Stop it, he ordered himself, forcibly tearing his gaze from the hard little peaks of Sommer's nipples where his T-shirt stretched tight across his chest. *You can fuck later, hopefully. Talk to him.*

It wasn't something Dean was used to thinking in relation to his sexual conquests. But Sommer was different. Damned if he knew why, and damned if he cared. The need to take the sadness out of Sommer's eyes superseded everything else.

"I could investigate your place," Dean offered, trying not to think of the scolding he was going to get from Kerry later. "If you want, I mean."

Sommer blinked at him. "You'd do that?"

"Sure."

"But you're only here for..." Sommer trailed off, his brows drawing together. "How much longer are you going to be here?"

"Eleven more days. That's plenty of time to chase your ghost for a while without neglecting Ron and Kerry." Stepping closer, Dean took Sommer's hand and flashed his most seductive smile. "Besides, that gives me an excuse to spend lots of time with you without looking desperate."

Sommer laughed. "All right, I'll take you up on it. I have to admit, it makes me feel better to know you'll be looking into my case." He leaned in and pressed a light kiss to Dean's lips. "Thank you, Dean."

"My pleasure." Dean flicked his tongue over Sommer's lips, enjoying the soft moan it drew from Sommer's throat. "Hey, Kerry, Ron and I were thinking we'd go play some Frisbee golf this afternoon. You want to come along?"

Sommer's expression clouded. "I'd love to, but I can't. I should be here when the guests show up."

Swallowing his disappointment, Dean smiled. "I totally understand. So when do you want me to come back and start investigating?"

The right corner of Sommer's mouth hitched up in that shy little half-smile that made Dean's heart thump. "There'll be enough staff here tomorrow evening that I'll be able to get away for a while. Why don't I take you out to dinner? We can talk about the investigation. Or whatever."

Warmth spread like a wave through Dean's body. Slipping both arms around Sommer's neck, he pressed closer. "That sounds fantastic."

"Great." Sommer's lips grazed the shell of Dean's ear. "I'll pick you up around five. We can go for a walk before dinner."

"Uh. Yeah. Okay." Dean shivered when Sommer's tongue traced a wet line up his neck. "Sommer, unless you're willing to fuck me right here in the woods, you'd better stop."

"Mmm." Sommer nipped Dean's earlobe. "I can't fuck you. No condom."

"Or lube." Dean canted his hips forward to rub his burgeoning erection against the fullness behind Sommer's

73

zipper. "Christ, Sommer. You're seriously turning me on here."

Sommer chuckled, his breath warm and damp on Dean's neck. "Am I?"

"You know you are."

"Hm." One of Sommer's hands slipped between Dean's legs to cup his swelling prick through his jeans. "Oh, yeah. You're really hard."

Dean just about came out of his skin when Sommer's fingers crept lower and gave his balls a hard squeeze. "Ah! Oh shit, you're gonna make me come if you keep that up."

With a couple of swift movements, Sommer flipped open the button of Dean's pants and tugged the zipper down. He plunged his hand inside Dean's underwear to wrap his fingers around Dean's shaft. "Come, then," he growled in Dean's ear.

Struck dumb, Dean could do nothing but stand there clinging to Sommer's shoulders and whimper while Sommer pumped his cock.

Between his powerful attraction to Sommer and the unexpected thrill of being jerked off just barely out of view of Sommer's back porch, it didn't take long for Dean to climax. He buried his face in Sommer's neck to stifle the cry he couldn't hold back as he coated Sommer's hand and both their clothes with semen.

When Dean's knees buckled, he didn't try to remain upright, but let himself slide out of Sommer's grip to crumple at his feet. Ignoring Sommer's concerned voice asking if he was okay, Dean undid Sommer's jeans, fished out his rigid prick and swallowed it whole.

Groaning, Sommer fisted both hands in Dean's hair. "Oh, my God. Yes."

His mouth full, Dean answered with a hum which made Sommer gasp and thrust down his throat. Dean would've grinned if he'd been able to. It felt deliciously dirty to kneel in the leaf mold on the forest floor, with his spent cock hanging out of his pants and Sommer's erection stretching his jaw open.

"Gonna come," Sommer panted, his fingers spasming in Dean's hair. "Oh God. Dean..."

Pulling off Sommer's cock, Dean closed one hand around the shaft and started stroking hard and fast. A second later, Sommer let out a hoarse moan, his prick pulsing in Dean's palm. Dean closed his eyes and smiled as Sommer's come painted his face. The sharp, musky smell made Dean's cock twitch in spite of his still-sated state.

With a deep, satisfied sigh, Sommer took Dean's hands and hauled him to his feet. "Wow. I've never done anything like that before."

"What, jerked a guy off?" Dean attempted to run a hand through his hair, and stopped when he encountered something wet and sticky. He laughed. "Well, just call me Mary."

Sommer blinked. "Huh?"

"You got spunk in my hair. It was all over your hand." Dean scraped a glob free and held it out. "See?"

Sommer looked startled, then burst out laughing.

"Oh. Like that movie."

"Yeah, like that movie." Dean licked his lips, savoring the taste of Sommer's semen. *Just a little won't hurt.* "I'm kind of a mess, aren't I?"

That sexy little half-smile curved Sommer's mouth. "You look good like this."

The roughness of Sommer's voice and the heat in his dark eyes made Dean's stomach flutter. He hid his reaction as best he could behind a teasing smile. It unnerved him how Sommer could turn him into a puddle with nothing but a look.

"Kinky bastard." Lifting the bottom of his shirt, Dean wiped his face clean. "So. You were saying you never jerked a guy off before? There's no way, man. I don't believe it."

"No, I have, just..." Sommer glanced around at the bare trees surrounding them. "Not like this. Outside, in the daytime. It feels different. More dangerous, or something."

"I hear you." Dean tucked his limp cock back into his jeans and zipped up, watching with an odd sense of loss while Sommer did the same. "It's the possibility of discovery, you know? It's exciting."

"Yeah. I've never felt the urge to act like that before, but I just couldn't seem to help myself." Framing Dean's face with his hands, Sommer stared into his eyes with an intensity that made Dean feel stripped bare. "You do very strange things to me, Dean. I think I like it."

Something deep in Dean's chest twisted. The way

Sommer looked at him made him feel vulnerable, yet protected at the same time. God, he'd never felt like this with anyone, never mind someone he'd only known for a few hours. It scared him to death.

Forcing his expression to remain bland, Dean drew Sommer's hands away from his face, leaned forward and pecked him on the lips. "Come on. Let's get back to the house before Kerry and Ron come looking for us."

Was it his imagination, or did disappointment flash through Sommer's eyes before his usual sweet smile took its place? "Yeah, okay. I have more work to do anyway before my guests arrive."

Sommer took Dean's hand and laced their fingers together. They walked back through the woods and toward the house in a silence which wasn't nearly as uncomfortable as Dean had expected it to be.

He couldn't help wondering what that meant, or if it meant anything at all.

♥

Dean told Ron and Kerry about his plans as soon as they arrived home. Kerry took it about as well as Dean had thought she would.

"You did *what*?"

Dean winced at Kerry's shrill tone. "I told Sommer I'd investigate his haunting. Just part-time," he added when he saw the disappointment in her eyes. "Just kind of informal, you know?"

Sighing, she plopped onto the living room sofa. "Well, I can't say I'm surprised."

"Me neither," Ron chimed in, strolling out of the kitchen with two bottles of beer. He handed Dean one and took a swig from the other. "You doing this because it's a cool haunted house case, or are you just looking to get laid?" He shot Dean an evil grin. "Again."

"Hey, I'm a professional. I'll only let him fuck me off the clock." Dean put the mouth of the beer bottle to his lips and took a long swallow.

Ron snickered. Kerry turned big, sad eyes to him. "Are you still gonna hang with us some?"

"Of course." Dropping onto the couch beside her, Dean pulled her into a one-armed hug. "Don't look like that, hon. I promise not to let the investigation take up too much of my time."

"What about Sommer?" She pulled back, watching his face. "I mean I like Sommer a lot, I really do, and I don't want to sound selfish, but I hope you don't spend all the rest of your visit with him."

Ron sprawled in the big, cushy chair across from the sofa. "Relax, babe. You'll get your Dean fix."

Kerry rolled her eyes at her husband's teasing grin. "Shut up."

"Y'all could help me investigate," Dean offered, ignoring for the moment the fact that he had no idea what they would actually do since he had no equipment other than his camera.

Ron's eyes lit up. "Oh man, that would be cool."

"It would. We've never done a paranormal investigation before." Kerry gave Dean a look halfway between cautious and hopeful. "You don't think Sommer would mind?"

"I can't imagine he would." Dean shrugged. "You know him better than I do, though, what do *you* think?"

"He won't care," Ron piped up before Kerry could answer. "So when do we start?"

Dean shook his head with a smile. Ron had always been one to jump into anything new with both feet. "Well, Sommer and I are going out tomorrow night to talk about the case—"

Kerry snorted. "Talk. Uh-huh. Sure."

"Talk about the case," Dean repeated, nudging Kerry's shoulder with his. "I guess we'll go from there, but I'm hoping I can really dig into it Tuesday, so let's tentatively plan on starting our investigation then."

"Sounds good." With a little squeal, Kerry grabbed Dean's arm in both hands and bounced in place. "Oh my God, this is exciting."

Dean laughed. "Wow, that was a quick turnaround. One minute you're mad at me, the next you're all excited."

"I wasn't mad," she protested, dropping Dean's arm.

"You were kind of mad," Ron interjected.

Kerry shrugged, a sheepish smile tugging at the corners of her mouth. "Okay, well, maybe a little. But it really is exciting to get to investigate a haunted house. I've always sort of wanted to. Plus this way, we get to spend more time with you."

"And I get to spend more time with y'all too." Leaning over, Dean kissed Kerry's cheek and stood. "Okay, since I have helpers now, I'm going to call Bo and see if he knows anyone local who can rent me some extra equipment."

"'Kay." Kerry heaved herself to her feet. "Well, since I can't have a beer like *some* people, I'm gonna go fix some tea."

Dean patted her back as he headed for the front door. Out on the small covered porch, he set his beer bottle on the arm of the porch swing and fished his cell phone out of his pocket. He sat in the swing and dialed Sam and Bo's home number.

He was about to give up and try later when Sam finally answered. "'Lo?"

Sam sounded distinctly out of breath. Dean grinned. "Hi, Sam. Did I interrupt something?"

"Not what you're thinking, no. We just got back from a run."

"How do you know what I was thinking? I know y'all run all the damn time for some unfathomable reason, maybe I already guessed that."

A snort sounded through the phone. "Somehow I doubt it."

"You know me too well, Sam." Dean picked up his beer and took a swig. "Could I talk to Bo for a sec? I want to ask him something."

"Yeah, sure, he's right here. It's good to talk to you, Dean."

"You too." Dean took a long swallow of beer while

waiting for Bo to come on the line.

A few seconds passed before Bo's voice came through the phone. "Hi, Dean. How are you?"

"I'm great. Having a fantastic time wallowing in nostalgia and making new friends."

Bo chuckled. "New friends, huh? Who have you seduced this time?"

"The owner of a local winery and bed and breakfast. He's hot, he's sweet and kind of shy, and he can really fuck a guy through the mattress."

Bo's laugh was louder this time, and Dean grinned at the mental image of Bo's inevitable blush. He set his beer down and cupped his crotch through his jeans. The thought of Sommer fucking him had his prick firming right up.

Down, Junior. You'll have to wait until tomorrow. He patted himself and retrieved his half-empty bottle so his hand wouldn't wander again.

"And that sort of brings me to the reason I called," Dean continued.

"You called to tell me about yet another man you're having a torrid sexual fling with?"

Bo sounded somewhere between horrified and amused, and Dean felt a flash of unreasonable anger. He knew quite well that everyone saw him as promiscuous, and he couldn't really argue that point when he bedded some new woman or man at least twice a month. But he hated hearing that knowledge in his friends' voices. It made him feel hollow and strangely tarnished.

"No," he said, keeping the sharpness out of his voice with an effort. "Sommer—that's the guy I was telling you about—has a haunted house. I told him I'd do an informal investigation there. Ron and Kerry are going to help me, so I was wondering if you knew anyone local who had equipment I could rent."

"Actually, yes, I do. The closest investigative group to you is in Raleigh, but I know a woman right there in Chapel Hill who sells most of the things you'd need. I'm sure she'll be happy to let you rent, just tell her you work for me and are investigating a local haunting." Bo hesitated a moment. "What sort of haunting is it?"

Dean bit back a laugh. Even after all the years he'd been in this business, Bo still got ridiculously excited about a new case. "I'm not entirely sure, but my gut says it's an honest-to-God apparition and not a residual."

"What makes you say so? Have you seen something?"

"Damn, Bo. **And** I thought Sam was the psychic one."

Soft, almost childlike laughter bubbled up through the phone. "Come on, Dean, what did you see?"

Bending one leg, Dean planted his foot on the swing and contemplated the small tear in the side of his sneaker. "Sommer, Kerry, Ron and I were in Sommer's kitchen earlier today, when a mist rose out of the floor and floated through the back door. Sommer and I followed it to a clearing in the woods behind his house, where it disappeared." He left out the part where Sommer got him off right there within sight of the house, as well as the part where he'd fallen to his knees and sucked Sommer's cock.

His prick stirred again, pressing against his zipper. Scowling, he adjusted himself and cursed his overactive libido.

"Hm. Well, it sure sounds like you might have an apparition there." Bo's excitement came through loud and clear. "Damn, I wish we could come up and do a full investigation."

"It's cool. I can manage, especially with Kerry, Ron and Sommer helping me out."

"How much time do you think you'll need?"

"Well, I'm only here for like eleven more days, so it can't very well take any longer than that."

"Would you like to stay a little longer?"

Dean blinked, surprised. "Um, well, yeah, actually, but—"

"Would two extra weeks be enough?"

Dean's mouth fell open. "What? Are you serious?"

"Yes. That would give you almost a month from today, is that long enough?"

"Yeah. Yeah, it is, but..." Dean chewed his bottom lip for a second. "Why?"

"You know as well as I do that real apparitions aren't exactly common. If that's really what your friend has, then it deserves more attention that you can give it in that short a time, especially since you'll be working part-time, with untrained personnel and rented equipment."

A slow smile spread over Dean's face. "I'd sure love to

stay longer, yeah. Thanks. You sure y'all can spare me?"

"I think so. Our caseload is light right now, thank God."

"Good. Okay, well, I guess I'm staying, then." Dean rubbed his thumb over the mouth of his beer bottle, grinning like a complete idiot. "I'll ask Sommer if we can publish some of the pics and video clips and stuff on the BCPI website. Assuming we get any worth publishing, that is."

"That would be wonderful."

"All right, cool. Oh, let me get the name and number of the lady with the equipment."

"Of course. Hang on a second, let me find it." There was a shuffle and a clunk which Dean assumed was Bo setting the phone down. Dean jumped up and ran inside, reaching the kitchen just as Bo came back on the line. "All right, I have it. Are you ready?"

Ignoring the puzzled look Kerry shot him from her spot at the kitchen table with her cup of tea, Dean grabbed the pen hanging from a string on the refrigerator and clicked it on. "Yeah, I'm ready."

He scribbled the name, address and phone number on the pad of paper held to the refrigerator door by a yin-yang magnet. The place was on a side street a couple of blocks off Franklin, not far from the middle of town. Maybe he and Sommer could go by there tomorrow before dinner.

I'm seeing him tomorrow.

A shiver of anticipation ran up Dean's spine.

Tomorrow didn't seem nearly soon enough. And wasn't it just kind of pathetic that he could get this worked up over someone he hadn't even known twenty-four hours yet?

"Dean? You still there?"

Shaking himself, Dean dropped the pen, tore off the page with the information on it and shoved it in his jeans pocket. "Yeah, I'm here. Hey, have I told you lately that you're the best boss in the world?"

"Every time I give you what you want, yes."

Dean laughed. "Thanks, Bo."

"You're welcome. Stay in touch, okay? Let us know how the investigation goes."

"I will. Bye."

"Bye."

Dean clicked off the phone, set it on the table and plopped into the chair across from Kerry, grinning. "Guess what."

She quirked an eyebrow at him over her teacup. "He gave you that pony you always wanted?"

"Goofball." He gave her leg a light kick under the table. "He was so excited about Sommer's possible apparition that he said I could stay here two extra weeks to do a better investigation."

Her eyes lit up. "Oh my God, that's *great!*"

"What's great?" Ron asked, coming out of the bathroom.

Kerry turned to him with a smile. "Dean's staying an extra two weeks to investigate Sommer's place."

Ron's face broke into a grin. "Awesome."

"Yeah. I'm pretty stoked about it." Putting the mouth of his bottle to his lips, Dean gulped down the rest of the liquid. "So. Are y'all still up for Frisbee golf?"

"Hell yeah." Kerry tossed back the rest of her tea, grabbed Ron's arm and levered herself to her feet. "I'm gonna kick your ass, Dean."

"You always do," Dean admitted ruefully. Kerry had a wicked arm when it came to tossing a Frisbee.

Chuckling, Ron patted Kerry's rounded belly. "Maybe you're gonna kick Dean's ass, but *I'm* gonna kick *your* ass."

"Ha. You wish."

"Babe, you're good, but you're not as good as me."

"Once again, you *wish.*"

Dean followed his friends out the back door, listening to their good-natured bickering with a smile on his face. He'd always admired their ability to squabble like a couple of overly competitive fifth graders without losing the glow they had only for one another.

Watching them made his gut burn with a sudden fierce longing. *I want that,* he thought, trailing Kerry across the grass to the car. *I want someone to look at me the way Ron and Kerry look at each other. I want someone to be the center of my world. I want...*

Dean stopped in mid-stride when he realized what he really wanted was to be in love. To feel that giddy joy whenever the person he loved was near. Only this time, he wanted the object of his affections to love him back in a way Sharon never had. The need was so strong he could almost picture a face in his head.

As a matter of fact, it was kind of a familiar face. He laughed out loud. Maybe all the freaky-ass cases Bay City Paranormal had handled lately had finally fried his brain.

Kerry turned to him with a frown. "What's so funny?"

"You and Ron. Y'all are so cute together." He figured it wasn't *really* a lie, since he'd been thinking exactly that only a few seconds earlier.

"Hm." She narrowed her eyes at him, obviously not buying it. "You sure you feel like playing today? You look awfully pale."

"Yeah, man, we can wait and go another time," Ron added, leaning across the roof of the car and eyeing him with concern.

"No, I'm fine, seriously." He shot them his most mischievous grin. "I'm pale from spending too much time indoors. So let's get out and get me some sunshine, huh?"

Ron laughed, and Kerry shook her head. "All right, don't tell us," she grumbled. Opening the car's passenger side door, she lowered herself into the seat. "Let's go. Loser buys the lattes at Open Eye."

"You're on." Dean pointed at her. "That's just the incentive I need to win this time."

She smirked over her shoulder as he slid into the backseat and shut the car door. "We'll see."

Dean let the teasing expression melt from his face when Kerry turned around. He rested the back of his head against the seat and stared out the window, wondering why the imaginary soul mate in his mind wore Sommer's lopsided smile.

Chapter Six

Dean woke before the sun Monday morning, feeling as if ants were crawling under his skin. It didn't take much thought to identify the cause of his uncharacteristic twitchiness. He was nervous about tonight.

Nervous. About going out with a man who'd already fucked him.

It was beyond weird. Dean hadn't been nervous about a date in ages and couldn't understand why he was now.

Maybe because you haven't actually been on a date with anyone but Kyle in so long, he mused, yawning while the coffee brewed.

He'd been with his last boyfriend, Kyle DuPree, for nearly six months before they broke up. They'd parted on friendly enough terms, considering, but Dean hadn't had a relationship last that long since his year with Sharon. It felt strange to be unattached again. He was out of practice when it came to dating.

Deep inside, though, he knew that his rusty dating skills weren't the cause of his pounding heart, or the fluttery feeling in his stomach. He liked Sommer. A lot. More than he should, really. That, he suspected, was the real reason for his current state of unrest.

"Pathetic, Dean," he muttered to himself. Taking a mug from the cabinet, he filled it with coffee, doctored it with chocolate soy creamer and prepared to face a long, unsettled day.

Dean lasted until almost lunchtime before he got to the point where he either had to get out and do something or explode. Ron was working, so Dean dragged Kerry downtown with him to find the shop Bo had told him about. Once she learned Dean was an employee of BCPI, the owner, Susan Unger, was happy to rent out all the equipment Dean needed. He and Kerry left the shop with two EMF detectors, two audio recorders, a thermal imaging camera and one stationary camera which would hook up to Dean's laptop.

By the time Sommer's dark green SUV pulled up in front of the house that evening, Dean was feeling calmer, thanks to keeping himself usefully occupied all afternoon in planning the upcoming investigation. "Sommer's here," he called to Ron and Kerry, who were in the family room in the back of the house watching TV. "I'm off. Don't wait up."

"Have fun," Ron answered.

"And call us if you're staying over," Kerry added.

Dean laughed. "Sure thing. Bye, y'all."

He bounded out onto the front porch and down the steps just as Sommer strolled around the front of the SUV and started toward him. A wide smile lit Sommer's face.

"Hi, Dean."

"Hi." Dean raked an appreciative gaze up and down Sommer's body. "Wow, you look hot."

Sommer's blush stained his cheeks nearly the color of the long-sleeved silk shirt hugging his upper body. "Thank you." Taking Dean's hand, he pulled him close and pecked him on the lips. "So do you."

"Thanks." Dean licked his lips. They tingled where Sommer had kissed him. "So, what's the plan? Where are we going?"

Sommer gave Dean's hand a squeeze before letting go so Dean could walk around the front of the SUV to the passenger side. "I thought we could go walk around downtown, go window-shopping or whatever, then go to Pepper's for dinner." He gave Dean a shy, sidelong look as he slid behind the wheel and Dean bounced into the passenger seat. "It's not fancy or anything, but the food's wonderful and I love the atmosphere there."

"Yeah, I remember Pepper's." Dean smiled at the memories of college evenings spent at the little downtown restaurant, sharing pizzas and pitchers of beer with his friends. "That sounds like fun to me."

"Good. I hoped you would approve." Reaching across the console, Sommer clamped a hand onto the back of Dean's neck. "Come here."

Dean leaned sideways to meet Sommer's mouth with his. He opened for Sommer's tongue, his head buzzing as if he was drunk. Sommer's fingers massaged his neck in gentle circles. He imagined he could feel every cell sparking in the wake of Sommer's touch.

When the kiss broke, Dean trailed his fingertips along Sommer's cheek as they pulled apart. "I like kissing you," he whispered. He didn't know why he felt the sudden need to tell Sommer that—there was no way in hell Sommer didn't already know—but he couldn't help it. He stared at the hollow of Sommer's throat, hoping he didn't sound as much like a kid with a crush as he was afraid he did.

"I like it too." Drawing back, Sommer lifted Dean's chin and stared into his eyes with unnerving intensity. "Will you come back home with me tonight, Dean? I'd very much like to have you in my bed again."

Dean swallowed the swarm of butterflies threatening to burst out of his chest. "Oh yeah. I'd fucking *kill* to have your cock up my ass again."

With a laugh, Sommer straightened up and cranked the engine. "No need for homicide. If you ever want me, all you have to do is say the word."

Dean grinned. "The word."

The sweet, crooked smile that made Dean's heart flutter curved Sommer's mouth. "If I fucked you right here in front of Kerry and Ron's house, Kerry would be the one committing murder."

"Good point." Dean shot a nervous glance at the front door. "Let's go."

"Absolutely." Sommer turned to check the road behind him, then pulled away from the curb and headed down the road toward downtown. "Anyway, we have a nice, comfortable, *private* bed waiting for us after dinner.

I'm sure we can both wait that long."

At the moment, Dean wasn't sure about that at all, but he wasn't about to say so. If Sommer could wait, he could too.

He hoped.

To his own surprise, Dean found that waiting wasn't as intolerable as he'd thought it would be. Strolling hand-in-hand down Franklin Street with Sommer gave him a faint euphoric buzz and laid a sheen of newness over the nostalgia he always felt when visiting Chapel Hill.

By the time they started toward Pepper's Pizza for dinner, Dean realized with a shock that he hadn't felt this relaxed with anyone in a long, long time. Even with Kyle, he'd invariably kept a part of himself back. The fact that Sommer had broken through his automatic guard without even trying was both exhilarating and terrifying.

They sat at a small, two-person booth in the back of the restaurant. Once they'd ordered their meals and the waiter had brought them each a glass of wine, Sommer finally brought up the subject which was the official reason for this outing. "So. Give me the crash course on paranormal investigation."

"What would you like to know?"

"I don't know. That is, I know so little about the subject that I have no idea what I don't know. If that makes any sense."

"Strangely enough, it does."

Sommer laughed. "I guess you should start at the

beginning, then. What's going to happen? How long will it take? And do I get to help, or should I just stay out of the way?"

Dean smiled at the spark of excitement in Sommer's eyes. "Well, what's basically going to happen is, we'll try to catch hard evidence of your ghost—video or audio—then analyze it. If we don't find a more mundane explanation for whatever we see or hear, then we can call it paranormal and go from there. As for how long it takes, well..." Dean bit his lip, nervous suddenly. What if Sommer didn't want him hanging around for a whole month?

"Yes?" Sommer prompted. "How long?"

Taking a sip of his wine, Dean gathered his courage and plowed on. "It sort of depends on the investigation, but I, um, I called my boss and he said I could stay here an extra two weeks to make sure I could do a thorough job, since it's just me and you, and Ron and Kerry too of course, and since I'm using my own camera plus Ron's and some rented equipment. Which means I'd be here nearly a month, and yeah, you can help."

Sommer gave him a shocked look. "You'll be investigating for a month? And using equipment?"

"Yes." Dean's heart plummeted into his feet at the expression on Sommer's face. *Shit, he doesn't want me to be around that long.* "I'm sorry, Sommer, I just thought... I mean, I...I don't have to. Bo—that's my boss—thought this case deserved that kind of time, and I agree, I mean you don't see a real apparition that often, and—"

Sommer reached across the table and laid his fingertips to Dean's lips, stopping his babbling. "In case you hadn't noticed, Dean, I like you. A lot. The idea of having you around for the next month is a very attractive one." He dropped his hand with a sigh. "But this sounds like it's turning into a professional job, and I don't have the money to pay you."

Ridiculously relieved, Dean wound his fingers through Sommer's and squeezed. "I'm going to do my level best to give you a pro-level investigation, but it's not a Bay City Paranormal job, and there's no charge. I'm doing this because I want to."

Sommer's teeth dug into his lower lip. "You're sure?"

"Yes." Dean leaned over the table, his thumb caressing Sommer's knuckles. "Listen, for a ghost geek like me your case is a fucking wet dream. Do you know how rare true apparitions are?"

"I'm guessing they're pretty rare." The corners of Sommer's mouth hitched up. "So you think that's what I have? An apparition?"

Dean shrugged. "There's no way to know for sure at this point, but it seems likely, yeah. Residual hauntings don't behave the way yours does."

Sommer tilted his head sideways, curiosity lighting his whole face. "What's a residual haunting, and how's that different from an apparition?"

"A residual is kind of like a recorded event. The same thing happens every time it's witnessed, often at the same time every day or month or whatever, and there's never any interaction with the witness or anyone else. An apparition is aware, intelligent—at least that's the theory—and able to communicate in some way with the living."

"Like leading a living person out to a certain spot in the woods."

"Possibly, yeah." Dean studied Sommer's face. "Do you know of any reason an apparition might be leading you into the woods?"

Sommer shook his head. "No, I don't. I can't imagine why there would be a ghost at the inn at all, never mind why it would be leading me anywhere."

"Hm." Picking up his wineglass with his free hand, Dean took a long swallow, thinking. "I know it's probably hard for you to talk about your parents, but do you know if they ever saw this apparition?"

"No, I don't have any idea. I wish I did." Sommer's gaze dropped to the dented wooden tabletop. "I barely even spoke to them for years before they disappeared. There's so much I don't know about them. Whether or not they ever saw my ghost is just one of those things."

Dean had no idea how to respond to that. He wanted to jump over the table and kiss away the sadness in Sommer's eyes, or at least say something comforting. But he couldn't think of a thing to say that didn't sound hollow and maudlin, and he didn't want to be too forward—*forward? He's had his cock up your ass, idiot, how's a kiss being forward?*—so he settled for lifting Sommer's hand and brushing his lips across the knuckles. The sweet smile he got in return told him he'd helped, even if it was only a little.

The arrival of bread and salads kept the silence from becoming awkward. Giving their waiter a smile, Dean let go of Sommer's hand to set a slice of hot, buttery garlic bread on Sommer's plate. He grabbed a piece for himself and bit into it. "Mmm. That's every bit as good as I remembered."

"Yeah. Sometimes when I'm in town I stop by here and get a bunch of garlic bread to take home." Sommer grinned. "All the baking I do, and my staff still likes Pepper's bread better than mine."

A thought struck Dean. "Hey, did any of your current employees work at the inn before you took over?"

"Just two, Rich Bates and Cody Selwyn. Rich has been the housekeeper ever since Blue Skye Inn opened, and Cody started at the winery a few months before my parents went missing." Picking up his wineglass, Sommer took a sip. "Why do you ask?"

"I was just thinking if any of the staff had been there since before you came on, maybe they could tell us if they or your folks had ever seen the ghost, or if anything else unusual had ever happened at the inn or the winery." Dean nibbled at the crust of his bread. "Is it all right with you if I talk to Rich and Cody, see if they know anything that'll help with this investigation?"

Sommer shrugged. "It's fine with me. I'll come with you, if that's okay."

"Sure. You don't have to, though. Unless you think

they won't talk to me or something."

"Rich might not unless I give him the go-ahead, actually. He's not exactly the most trusting person. It'll probably help if I'm either there with you, or at least tell him you're all right to talk to."

"Gotcha." Dean ran a fingertip around the rim of his wineglass. "What about Cody? I remember him, he waited on Ron, Kerry and me at Karaoke Night. Seemed like a nice kid."

"Oh, he is. Very friendly. He'll talk to you. The thing is, he'll flirt if you're alone with him, and, well..." Sommer hunched his shoulders, looking embarrassed. "I don't want anyone else coming on to you."

Normally, Dean had no use for jealous lovers. He rarely tied himself to an exclusive relationship, and when he did he expected mutual trust and respect, not a grip so tight he couldn't breathe. But something about the shine in Sommer's eyes made Dean feel safe rather than smothered.

Rising to one knee in his seat, Dean leaned across the table and planted a soft kiss on Sommer's lips. "He can flirt all he wants. It won't make me any more interested."

Sommer's fingers trailed along Dean's cheek as he settled back into the padded booth. "No?"

"No." Dean grinned. "Cody's a cute kid, but he's not my type. You, on the other hand? *So* are."

"Does that mean I can come with you to interview him?"

"Of course you can. I would've wanted you to anyhow,

you know. Blue Skye's your place, I'm sure you can think of things to ask that I wouldn't even realize we needed to know."

Sommer flashed his adorably crooked smile. "Good."

Their gazes locked, and something indefinable shifted between them. Dean's heart turned over hard. Whatever was happening here, it was happening fast. *Too* fast. But it felt so damn good to have someone look at him the way Sommer was looking at him now. Like he was more than just a good fuck.

Like he was special.

Kyle had looked at him that way, for a while. Until things had begun to move past casual and into serious, and Kyle had started to want things Dean couldn't give him.

Real commitment. His open and unshuttered heart.

He couldn't blame Kyle for leaving. He'd even been relieved, in a way, because the thought of giving himself completely to another person terrified him.

The paralyzing fear he'd felt when Kyle had said those three little words to him—the words he couldn't return, in spite of his loneliness and his longing to love someone—thumped through his blood now. This time, though, the thing making his palms sweat and his pulse race was the awareness that he *wanted* to bare his soul for Sommer, something he hadn't felt since Sharon left him. The need was so strong his body felt inadequate to contain it.

"Dean? Are you okay?"

Giving himself a mental shake, Dean met Sommer's

concerned expression with a smile which he hoped didn't look as forced as it felt. "Fine. Just planning in my head, you know?"

"Yeah." Sommer's hand covered his and squeezed. "I'm really excited about this investigation, Dean. Thank you for doing this."

"My pleasure, believe me."

Silence. Dean counted seven heartbeats before Sommer cleared his throat, slid to the edge of his seat and stood. "I'm going to the restroom. Be back in a minute."

"I'll be here." Dean winced. *Smooth, idiot.*

The corner of Sommer's mouth hitched up. Bending down, he brushed his lips over the shell of Dean's ear. "Call Kerry. Tell her you'll be at my place all night, getting fucked until you can't walk straight."

Oh my fucking God. Dean licked his lips. "Um. Yeah. 'Kay."

"Good." Sommer flicked Dean's earlobe with his tongue, then straightened up. "We wouldn't want her to worry."

Dean watched, dry-mouthed and painfully turned on, as Sommer strolled toward the bathroom. Sommer shot him a wicked smile before disappearing through the restroom door.

Letting out a breath he hadn't realized he'd been holding, Dean slumped in his seat. *Christ, he's gonna kill me.*

He dug his cell phone out of his pocket, flipped it open and dialed Kerry and Ron's number. "Kerry? Yeah, it's me. Sommer wanted me to tell you something..."

Chapter Seven

"All right, y'all settle down and let's go over the plan for tonight."

The chatter died down and three pairs of expectant eyes turned to Dean. He shook his head, grinning. Ron, Kerry and Sommer had been as excited as a bunch of kids on Christmas all evening. Who knew they'd harbored such a strong desire to be ghost hunters?

Strolling over to Sommer's parlor sofa, Dean sat between Sommer and Kerry and studied the checklist in his hand. "Okay, it's almost nine now. If we get started in the next few minutes, we'll have..." Dean counted silently in his head. "About four hours before we have to lay off for the night."

"We could actually keep going until two if we need to." Sommer slid a hand onto Dean's thigh, thumb rubbing tiny circles on his jeans. "My guests won't be here until around four o'clock tomorrow afternoon."

"How many?" Kerry asked, fiddling with her video camera.

"Just one couple. And they're the only ones scheduled this whole week." Sommer sighed. "I swear, business at the inn just keeps getting worse. I'm thinking of closing it down and trying to make it with just the winery."

Ron leaned forward in his chair, which sat catty-corner to the sofa. "That's probably a good idea. I'm betting the winery makes you more money anyhow, and with the inn closed you'd have more time to devote to winemaking."

"Yeah." Kerry's eyes lit up. "Hey, maybe you could do other stuff like Karaoke Night. Like have wine-tasting parties or something."

Sommer turned to her with a wide smile. "That's a fantastic idea. I'll have to look into that."

Kerry beamed, clearly pleased with herself. Dean laughed. "It *is* a great idea, but right now we have ghosts to bust. So let's get going." Leaning against Sommer's shoulder, Dean resumed reading his checklist. "Okay. Ron and Kerry, y'all take Kerry's video camera, one of the EMF detectors and one of the audio recorders. Sommer and I will take the other EMF and audio and the thermal imaging camera. We'll start with the downstairs, y'all start upstairs, then we'll switch. Video first, then EVP work. The lights are off everywhere but here, right?"

"Yes," Sommer said. "Upstairs, downstairs, outside, everywhere."

"Great, thanks. Y'all ready, then?"

They all nodded. Dean smiled, pleased. He'd spent about half an hour when he, Ron and Kerry arrived at the inn explaining about electromagnetic fields and electronic voice phenomena and showing his newly appointed assistants how to work the equipment. All three had picked it right up, much to his relief. He knew he wasn't much of a teacher, despite Kerry's assurances to the contrary.

Giving Sommer's hand a quick squeeze, Dean pushed to his feet, wincing a little at the twinge in his backside. He and Sommer had spent an active couple of hours testing the sturdiness of Sommer's mattress the previous night after dinner, followed by a few hours of rest then another round in the shower. Dean had returned to Ron and Kerry's around noon, sore and bruised and practically floating. Funny how sex with Sommer energized him more than even the deepest sleep.

Ron grabbed his shoulder, making him jump. "Hey, should we take some still shots too? Kerry's video camera does stills."

Dean nodded. "Yeah, that's a good idea. Y'all do that."

"Okay." With a swift glance at Sommer, Ron patted Dean's back. "Try not to get too distracted, stud."

"Hey, I'm a professional," Dean protested as Ron wandered off, cackling, to collect his and Kerry's equipment. "Smartass."

Kerry pinched Dean's butt on the way to the stairs. "Just keep it in your pants, both of you. Ghosts always show up when you're not looking."

Dean shook his head at Ron and Kerry as they trooped up the steps. "I swear, neither of them ever matured past eighth grade. I worry for that poor kid."

Chuckling, Sommer sidled up behind Dean and

wrapped both arms around his waist. "Why do I think they'd say the same thing about you?"

"Probably because they would. Except for the kid part."

"Yeah, except for that." Sommer grabbed Dean's hips and spun him around. "Quick, kiss me before the ghost shows up."

Oh, hell yeah. Dean pressed close, tilted his face up and kissed Sommer's smiling mouth. Sommer opened to him with a soft moan that made his skin sizzle.

"I guess we should start working at some point," Sommer murmured when they eventually drew apart.

"Mmm. Yeah, probably." Reluctantly pulling out of Sommer's arms, Dean plucked the EMF detector and audio recorder from the coffee table and handed it to Sommer. "Keep the EMF meter and audio recorder running. I'll do the thermal imaging. We can both ask questions when we do EVP work."

"All right." Sommer switched both pieces of equipment on and grinned at Dean. "I'm all set."

Dean grinned back, his stomach turning somersaults. God, but Sommer's smile did things to him. "Let's start with this room, since we're here already. Then we'll go in order counterclockwise. Dining room, kitchen, your bathroom and bedroom, then the foyer."

"And we're leaving the stationary camera in the kitchen running all night, right?"

Dean nodded. "Yeah. It's set up with a wireless connection to my laptop." He gestured toward the iBook on the coffee table. "We don't have enough people to monitor it continuously, but that's okay. Whenever anyone's in here we can check on it and see what's going on, at least. And the entire night's video'll be recorded on my laptop."

"Sounds good."

Dean glanced at his watch, which he'd synchronized earlier with the thermal camera and audio. "This is Dean and Sommer, Tuesday January tenth, two thousand and six, nine oh two p.m., Blue Skye Inn parlor. Date, time and place for the record," he explained in answer to Sommer's puzzled expression.

"Ah. Okay." Sommer held up the EMF meter. "EMF is zero point one."

"Walk around the room with it. Make a slow, steady circuit, and see if there's any spikes anywhere."

Sommer paced along the wall, his gaze glued to the backlit EMF detector. Dean switched off the light, then stood in front of the coffee table, turning in a slow circle to capture the entire room on video. Sommer's form blazed red and orange on the screen as Dean scanned past him. Dean lingered on the brilliantly colored curves of Sommer's ass for a moment before moving on.

Other than a minimal spike in EMF around the TV and stereo, the parlor yielded nothing of interest. Neither did the dining room. Dean had high hopes for the kitchen, since that was where Sommer had always seen the apparition before, but it was just as quiet as the other downstairs rooms. By the time he and Sommer trudged upstairs to switch areas with Ron and Kerry—who hadn't seen or heard anything either—Dean had resigned himself to an experience-free night. Those tended to be the rule rather than the exception, but he'd hoped to see something tonight, mostly so his friends could feel the heart-pounding rush of a personal paranormal encounter backed up by video or audio.

Oh well, we have nearly a month to investigate. There's plenty of time.

"Entering guestroom four," Dean announced for the record as he and Sommer walked into the second-to-last upstairs room. "Sommer? Anything?"

"Not really. EMF's zero point four, a little higher than it's been up until now but—" He stopped, staring hard at the meter. "Wait a sec, it's going up. Zero point seven, one point one, one point six." He looked up, frowning. "Is it just me, or is it cold in here?"

"You're right, it is."

"Does that mean the ghost is near?"

"Maybe." Dean turned the thermal camera toward Sommer, scanning the area around him. "Ask some questions, like is anyone here, who is it, what do they want, stuff like that. Leave a few seconds in between questions so if anything's here it'll have a chance to answer without us talking over it."

"Okay." Sommer licked his lips. "Uh. Is there anyone here with us?" He paused, his eyes wide in the darkness. "What's your name?"

On the thermal screen, a grayish blue form

materialized about a foot to Sommer's left. A thrill of excitement shot up Dean's spine. "Don't panic, but there's a figure right next to you."

Sommer drew in a sharp breath. His shoulders tensed. "Where?"

"To your left."

Moving slowly, Sommer reached out his left hand. It plunged right into the heart of the nebulous shape. "It's colder here. Like ice. It's making my hand numb."

"You've got your hand right inside it." The thing began floating away. "Hang on, it's moving." Dean glanced at Sommer, who stood frozen to the spot, staring at the faint mist Dean could now see wafting across the room. "Looks like it's headed for the dresser."

"Oh, my God." Sommer's voice was an awed whisper. "Who are you? What are you trying to tell us?"

Dean got the distinct feeling that Sommer wasn't doing EVP work this time. The questions sounded less like prompts and more like pleas for something to help him understand.

Keeping one eye on the thermal, Dean moved to Sommer's side and kissed his shoulder. "Is there something you need to show us?" Dean asked, staring at the misty shape on the camera's screen.

As he and Sommer watched, the form sank into the front of the dresser. The bottom right drawer rattled halfway open.

Sommer let out a gasp. "Oh my God, Dean. Did that drawer just open by itself?"

"Yes." Dean shot a swift glance at Sommer. "Is this room used for anything besides guests?"

"Not anymore, no."

"Anymore? Does that mean it was at some point?"

"Yes. This used to be my mother's sewing room." Sommer walked forward and laid a hand on the dresser, as if expecting it to feel different. On the camera's screen, his hand glowed red against the darkness of the cool wood. "I converted it to a guestroom just last year. I don't know why. I sure as hell didn't need the space, even then, I just... It reminded me of her, and how she and Dad never came back."

The resigned sorrow in Sommer's voice tore at Dean's heart. He studied the thermal screen. The form, whatever it was, hadn't returned. It seemed to have vanished. Crossing to where Sommer still stood with one hand on the dresser, Dean set the camera on the solid surface and wound his arms around Sommer's waist. "Are you okay? We can stop if you want."

Nodding, Sommer looped his arms around Dean's neck, the equipment still in his hands. "I'm fine. My folks and I haven't been close for a long time, but they're my parents and I love them. It's hard, not knowing what happened to them, whether they're dead or alive." He laughed, the sound soft and sad. "It'd almost be easier if they were dead. At least that way, there'd be a damn good reason why they never contacted me."

Dean nuzzled into Sommer's hair. "I'm sorry."

Turning his head, Sommer brushed a light kiss across

Dean's temple. "It's all in the past now. Let's see what's in this drawer."

Dean blinked. For a moment there, he'd forgotten all about the mysteriously opened drawer and what it might mean for the investigation. He gave Sommer a squeeze, then dropped his arms and pulled his mini flashlight out of his pocket. "You want me to look, or would you rather?"

In answer, Sommer set the EMF detector and audio recorder on top of the dresser and held out his hand. Dean put the flashlight in Sommer's palm. Sommer switched it on and knelt on the floor beside the dresser. While he carefully pulled the drawer fully open and shone the light inside, Dean picked up the camera and aimed it at Sommer. "Is there anything there?"

"I don't see anything." Bending lower, Sommer aimed the flashlight's beam and peered into the depths of the drawer. He ran his free hand along the inside and along the underside, then straightened up with a sigh. "It's empty. Nothing attached to the bottom either."

"I'm impressed that you even thought to look there. I wouldn't have."

"Yeah, well, I always wanted to be a detective when I was a kid. I had the entire Hardy Boys collection. Used to drive my family and friends crazy tapping on the walls all the time, looking for hollow spots and secret passages."

The mental image of a wide-eyed and serious young Sommer, hunting for hidden doorways and forgotten secrets, made Dean smile. "That's adorable."

"Too bad my childhood detecting skills didn't pay off

this time." Sommer clambered to his feet, his mouth hitching into the crooked smile that made Dean's chest ache. He pushed the drawer shut with his foot, turned off the flashlight and stuck it in the back pocket of his jeans. "We have one more room left. Is it all right if we move on?"

"Sure." Dean glanced around the room. He saw nothing resembling the misty figure from before, and nothing showed on the thermal. "Even if nothing else happens, I think we got some really strong evidence with the thermal. Who knows, maybe we'll get something on audio too."

"I hope so." Retrieving the EMF detector and audio recorder, Sommer walked to the doorway with Dean beside him. Sommer stopped in the hallway and stared into the darkness of the spacious room. "I wonder why that...that apparition, or whatever it was, wanted us to see an empty drawer?"

"That's a very good question." Dean studied Sommer's face in the cool glow of the thermal screen. "Was the dresser there before you converted the room to a guestroom?"

"Oh, yeah. The drawers were full of my mom's sewing supplies." Sommer smiled. "The one we just looked at was packed so full of patterns I almost couldn't get it open. I remember that because two of the patterns tore when I finally forced the drawer open, and I felt bad about ruining her things."

Dean moved closer and hooked his free arm around Sommer's waist. "That's all there was, though? Sewing supplies?"

"Yes. I went through every bit of it, hoping to find some sort of clue about where Mom and Dad had gone, but there was nothing."

"I'm assuming you've never experienced anything like what just happened, or you would've said so."

"No, I haven't. On the other hand, I haven't been in this room since I first converted it. Rich does the cleaning here." Sommer chewed his bottom lip. "I just don't like being here. I know that sounds weird."

Moved by the urge to quell Sommer's obvious embarrassment, Dean pressed a soft kiss to Sommer's neck. "It doesn't sound weird at all, actually. I think I'd feel the same way, if it was me."

Turning, Sommer kissed Dean's lips. "Thank you," he whispered. "You always make me feel better."

Warmth flared in Dean's belly. He couldn't have stopped the loopy smile from spreading across his face even if he'd wanted to. "Hey, anything I can do. I like making you feel good."

The sudden heat in Sommer's eyes told Dean he'd caught the double meaning. Not that it wasn't painfully obvious.

"Let's finish this up," Sommer breathed. "Before I have to molest you right here in the hall."

Dean gulped. "Uh. Yeah. As long as you promise to molest me later."

Sommer drew away, but his gaze held Dean's. "Stay with me."

Ignoring the fact that Kerry was likely to complain

about him spending so much time with Sommer, Dean nodded. The simmering fire in Sommer's eyes promised pleasures Dean was too weak to refuse.

A wide smile lit up Sommer's face. "Good."

Sommer started toward the last room, his attention fixed on the EMF once more. Dean followed on rubbery legs. It was both irritating and exciting how Sommer could destroy his composure with nothing but a look and a few words.

Remember the case, Dean. Stop fantasizing about Sommer and concentrate on the damn case.

With a mighty effort, Dean forced his thoughts away from sex and onto the mystery of the Blue Skye Inn. The opening of the dresser drawer nagged at his mind. In his experience, apparitions did not expend the energy to deliberately draw the attention of the living without a reason. Not that their reasons were always clear, but they did always seem to have one.

Something's still there in that drawer, or was there before Sommer cleaned it out. Some clue to who or what this apparition is. We just have to figure out what it is.

A pleasant shiver pebbled the skin of Dean's arms, and he smiled. It was going to be an interesting month.

Chapter Eight

The last guestroom yielded nothing but a large moth fluttering against the window. Dean and Sommer descended the stairs and went into the parlor, where Ron and Kerry sat talking on the sofa. The lamp they'd turned on filled the room with a golden glow.

Both looked up when Dean and Sommer came in and set their equipment on the coffee table. "Hey," Kerry said. "Did y'all find anything? We didn't get squat."

Dean plopped into one of the huge, squashy chairs. Sommer perched on the arm. His fingers sifted through Dean's hair, and Dean swallowed a moan. "Um. Most of the house was totally quiet for us. Something happened in room four upstairs though."

Ron leaned forward, practically vibrating with curiosity. "What?"

Dean explained what they'd experienced in the guestroom, with occasional interjections from Sommer. By the time he finished, Kerry's eyes were huge and Ron was actually bouncing in place.

"That is so *fucking* wild." Ron rubbed at his beard. "So what do you think it was trying to show you?"

Sommer shook his head. "I don't know. But this doesn't end here. I'm going to go back up there tomorrow and search the whole dresser. The whole room, if I have to. There *has* to be something there, and I'm not giving up until I find it."

The steely determination in Sommer's voice made Dean's cock swell inside his jeans. He bit his lip and tried to will it down. God, Sommer's aggressive side turned him on even when it wasn't sexual.

He wished it wouldn't. It unnerved him that anyone— never mind a man he barely knew—could exert so much control over him without even trying.

But it could be fun, his inner hedonist whispered. *Just think of it. Sommer dominating you. Controlling you. I bet he could make you come with nothing but his voice.*

The mental picture was too damn tempting. Dean cleared his throat and blinked away the fog of desire blurring his vision. He cringed inwardly at Kerry's suspicious stare and Ron's knowing smirk. "Um. Okay. Well. The camera's set up in the kitchen, it'll run all night, and, uh, well, I guess we'll come back and do more investigating Thursday night."

"That sounds good," Sommer said, sounding infuriatingly calm. "Ron, Kerry, I hope you don't mind if Dean stays with me again tonight. I'll drive him home in the morning, along with all the equipment. I wish I could help y'all review the evidence, but I'll be too busy tomorrow."

Kerry sighed. "Fine. Y'all just make sure you actually

sleep at some point. Otherwise neither of you'll be any good for what you need to do tomorrow."

Dean couldn't answer. Sommer's hand had slid down his back, one finger dipping below the waist of his jeans to caress bare skin, and Dean felt as if all the blood in his body had gone zooming into his crotch. He swallowed.

Snickering, Ron stood. "Come on, babe. Let's head on home. You need to get some rest after running all over the house all night."

"I'm fine," she protested as Ron took her hands and tugged her to her feet. "Dr. Chavez said I can still do everything I normally do, I don't need any extra rest."

"Okay, well, it's late and I have to work in the morning."

"But, Ron—"

Ron silenced her with a kiss. "Kerry. Unless you want to watch Dean and Sommer fuck, we really need to go."

"Oh, God," Sommer muttered, covering his face with the hand which had previously been worming its way down between Dean's butt cheeks.

"Okay, okay." Kerry giggled. "Not that I wouldn't give a limb to watch, guys, but yeah, I think we'll just leave now."

Jumping up, Sommer followed Ron and Kerry to the door. "Thank you both for helping out tonight."

"It was fun." Ron clapped Sommer on the shoulder. "'Night, Sommer." He leaned sideways and grinned at Dean. "'Night, Dean."

Dean managed a smile and a wave. "See y'all tomorrow."

As soon as Ron and Kerry left, Sommer turned and pinned Dean with a smoldering look. Dean watched, pulse racing, as Sommer stalked toward him across the room. God, but the man was too sexy for his own good. Dean wished his legs would work so he could get up, tackle Sommer to the floor and ravish him.

When Sommer reached Dean's chair, he fisted a hand in Dean's hair, bent and kissed him hard. Dean opened wide for Sommer's tongue. By the time Sommer broke the kiss, Dean felt weak and dizzy. He stared into Sommer's face from inches away, wishing he could make his voice work.

Sommer growled, his hand still clenched in Dean's hair and lust blazing in his eyes. "Take your clothes off."

Dean went straight for the buttons on his shirt. He couldn't remember why he'd even worn something with buttons in the first place. He'd known all along—or hoped, at least—that the night would include sex. Yet he'd worn the snug green Oxford-style silk instead of an easy-to-remove sweater, just because it emphasized the lean muscles in his back.

Right now, it hardly seemed like a worthwhile trade.

He let out a frustrated mewl when his shaking fingers slipped for the third time. Undressing was going to take forever at this rate.

Before he could get his brain functioning well enough to ask for help, Sommer balled the hem of Dean's shirt in both hands and pulled the whole thing over his head. Dean heard the fabric rip. A button bounced off his lap and onto the floor.

"Sorry," Sommer mumbled, hauling Dean to his feet and crushing their bodies together.

"'S okay." Dean arched his neck so Sommer could suck the tender spot just at the curve of his shoulder. He grabbed Sommer's shoulder hard with one hand and stuck the other down the back of Sommer's jeans. "God. Bedroom, Sommer, fuck."

Sommer shook his head. His hair tickled Dean's neck. "No. Here."

Need flared white-hot up Dean's spine and into his skull. His hands moved of their own accord to shove Sommer's long-sleeved T-shirt up. He got distracted by a rosy nipple and stopped to suck on it for a moment while Sommer tore the shirt over his head and threw it on the floor.

Sommer managed to undo Dean's pants while he was busy kneading Sommer's ass and decorating his throat with purple marks. Dean only noticed his jeans had been lowered when he felt Sommer's fingers curl around his cock. He moaned into Sommer's neck.

Dean felt his head yanked back by the hair, and Sommer's mouth descended on his. Sommer's tongue forced Dean's jaw wide. Dean yielded gladly, fumbling Sommer's jeans open and shoving a hand inside to grasp his cock as the kiss turned rough and desperate.

When Sommer's fingers delved lower to slide along the

sensitive skin behind Dean's balls, his knees nearly buckled. Sommer seemed to take that as his cue. Prying Dean's fingers off his shaft, he spun Dean around, dragged him sideways a few feet and bent him across the arm of the chair.

Sommer leaned over Dean's back, molding their bodies together. His cock nestled hot and rigid between Dean's buttocks. Dean whined and pressed backward. The need to have Sommer's prick inside him was so strong he couldn't think of anything else.

A low groan rumbled into Dean's ear. "I love how much you want me." Sommer's hand curled around Dean's cock once more, thumb caressing the slit. Dean keened and clawed the chair. "I love how hard you are for me."

In a tiny coherent corner of his brain, Dean marveled at Sommer's control. Dean felt shattered into a million pieces, torn apart by his own desire. He envied Sommer's ability to keep it together.

Sommer's warm weight left Dean's back. He flailed a hand behind him, trying to keep Sommer in place. "No. Fuck me now."

"I think I have some lube and rubbers in the entertainment center drawer, I'm just going to get them. I'll be right back." Soft hair brushed Dean's shoulder blade, and Sommer's lips pressed briefly to his back. "Don't move."

The command held just enough steel to keep Dean firmly in place, his bare ass in the air and his erection pressed into the smooth maroon fabric of the chair's arm. If he lifted his head a little and turned to the right, he'd be able to see the stripe of blackness where the heavy drapes didn't quite meet in the middle. The sliver of potential exposure sent a jolt of excitement through him.

He was rubbing against the chair and imagining someone out on the porch watching him and Sommer fuck when a hand on his butt announced Sommer's return. "You didn't start without me, did you?"

Dean shivered at the faint whiff of reprimand underlying the amusement in Sommer's voice. He shook his head.

"Good."

The sound of a condom packet being torn open came from behind Dean. He heard the faint rustle as Sommer put on the rubber, then a snap and a squelch followed by a swift shock of cold lube on his anus. The gel warmed fast with the friction of Sommer's fingers slipping inside Dean, twisting and pumping to stretch him.

"God, you feel so good," Sommer murmured. "I can't wait to be inside you."

Then do it! Dean's mind screamed. *Fuck me already.*

All that came out was a pitiful whine. Frantic, he rocked backward, deliberately clenching his hole around Sommer's fingers. Sommer sucked in a hissing breath. His hand withdrew. Dean had a split second to brace himself before Sommer's cock slammed into him.

"Oh fuck yeah," Dean gasped, the words knocked loose by the force of Sommer penetrating him. He squeezed his eyes shut against the spike of pleasure-pain. "Hard. Fuck me hard."

Getting a firm grip on Dean's hipbones, Sommer pounded into him so hard his teeth clacked together. "God. Dean."

Sommer's words emerged in a rough whisper which started a hot, fierce ache deep in Dean's chest. He didn't know if the obvious lust did it for him, or the more subtle tenderness, but either way Dean liked it. Moaning, he dug his fingers into the seat of the chair and angled his body so that Sommer's cock hit his gland with every thrust.

With a growl that set Dean's blood on fire, Sommer picked up the pace. His fingers gripped Dean's hips hard enough to bruise, his prick stretched Dean's hole and pummeled his prostate, and it was more than Dean could withstand. Overwhelmed by sensation, Dean came with a loud wail.

Behind him, Sommer let out a sharp cry. "Fuck, oh, oh *fuck*." He thrust into Dean a few more times, then went still. His cock pulsed in Dean's ass, his hands spasmed, and Dean grinned. He *loved* it when Sommer came inside him. Was already addicted to the rush, in fact. The only thing that would make it better was if he could feel Sommer's semen trickling out of his ass.

Sommer draped himself over Dean's back with a contented sigh. "Wow."

Dean reached a hand back to tangle in Sommer's silky hair. "You can say that again."

"Okay." Shifting a little, Sommer nipped Dean's

earlobe. "Wow. Seriously. Wow."

Dean laughed, jostling Sommer's cock inside him. He clamped down to hold it in place, making Sommer jerk and hiss. "You planned this."

"What, having sex with you?" Sommer planted a kiss on Dean's bare shoulder. "Guilty."

"No, not that." Twisting around as much as he could with Sommer's weight holding him down, Dean tugged Sommer's face down for a real kiss. "I mean, you planned to fuck me in here. Right over this chair, I'm thinking."

"Well, it *is* the right height."

"This is true."

"Mmm." Sommer kissed Dean again, then peeled himself off Dean's back. "So. Now that phase one of my evil plan has come to fruition—"

"Phase one?" Dean squeaked as Sommer pulled out of him.

"Fucking you in the parlor." Sommer smacked Dean's ass hard. "Don't interrupt."

Grinning, Dean straightened up and turned to face Sommer. "Yessir."

"Good boy." The used condom clutched between two fingers, Sommer snaked his free arm around Dean's waist and pulled him close. "As I was saying, now that phase one has been accomplished, why don't we move on to phase two?"

"Which is?" Dean tilted his head to brush Sommer's mouth with his.

Sommer's tongue flicked out, teasing the corner of Dean's mouth. "Fucking in the bedroom, like normal people."

Dean's cock twitched. *Damn.* Nobody had gotten his libido this worked up in years. He licked his lips. "I like that plan."

"Thought you might." Sommer kissed his nose, gave his butt a hard squeeze and let go. "Go to the bedroom, get undressed and lie face down on the bed. I'll be there in a minute."

Dean's knees went wobbly. He reached out to steady himself on the chair behind him. God, it was hot when Sommer got bossy like that. "Where are you going?"

"To throw this away." Sommer held up the semen-filled rubber. "Then I need to clean off the chair."

Dean turned, saw the sticky mess on the chair and winced. "Sorry."

"Don't be. It was *my* plan, remember?" Leaning over, Sommer pecked him on the lips. "So. After that, I need to go get a few things. It won't take long."

"Things?"

An evil grin spread across Sommer's face. "My toy collection."

Something told Dean Sommer wasn't talking about action figures. His cock jerked. "Um. Toys. Yeah."

Laughing, Sommer tugged Dean's jeans up with one hand and gave him a gentle push in the direction of the foyer. "Bed, Dean. Go."

Dean obediently wandered across the parlor and through the foyer toward Sommer's bedroom. He couldn't help wondering how smart it was to let a relative stranger use God only knew what sorts of toys on him. But instinct told him to trust Sommer. To listen to the part of him that felt safer with Sommer than he'd ever felt with anyone.

Listen to your gut, he told himself. *It's smarter than your brain sometimes.*

Grinning, he sauntered into Sommer's room and started pulling off his clothes.

♥

Dean lay sprawled face down on Sommer's kitchen table, naked, wrists and ankles secured to the wooden legs by black yarn. Dildos, butt plugs and cock rings littered the floor. In the corner, a misty white shape sat at a sewing machine, busily stitching together bits of multicolored fabric. The sky outside the window blazed red.

Suddenly Dean felt Sommer's presence behind him. Sommer touched him, hands spreading his ass cheeks apart. Electricity skated over his skin, and he moaned.

"Are you ready for my toy?" Sommer purred, his breath warm on the back of Dean's neck.

Robbed of speech, Dean whimpered and lifted his hips. Cool, hard plastic penetrated him. Plastic legs, plastic hips, plastic torso. He could almost see the muscular plastic arms and square-jawed plastic head sticking out of his ass. Odd lumps and ridges rubbed his insides as Sommer pumped the doll in, out, in again. It felt so good Dean's entire body ached with it. He moaned Sommer's name.

"You're beautiful, Dean." Sommer branded the curve of Dean's lower back with a kiss. "So beautiful. Dean. Dean..."

"Dean! Wake up."

Dean's eyes flew open. "What? I'm awake."

"Yeah, *now* you are." Kerry set a huge yellow mug on the table in front of Dean, then sat in the chair beside him and lifted her own mug. "Should you really be reviewing evidence when you can't even stay awake?"

Dean blinked the fuzziness from his eyes and tried to focus on the laptop screen. At least he'd managed to pause the video before he fell asleep. "I'm just a little tired, that's all. The coffee'll help, thanks."

"You're welcome." Kerry gave him a considering look as he sipped the hot, fragrant liquid. "So. What were you dreaming about?"

The dream-memory of a toy up his ass—an *actual* toy, not the plugs and clamps and other things whose residual ache he still felt—made Dean choke on his coffee. "Um. You don't want to know, trust me."

"I'll take your word for it." She took a swallow of coffee, peering at Dean over the top of the mug. "So. You've been home for like two hours, but I still haven't seen that video."

He thought of the short but sizzling clip Sommer had taken on his digital camera just this morning and nearly dropped his coffee on the floor. "Um. What video?"

"The video from last night, genius. From the

investigation? The video with the *ghost* on it?"

"Oh yeah. That." Hunching his shoulders, he drank deeply from his mug. "Sorry. I'm just really tired."

"Obviously." She grinned at him. "You and Sommer must've had some night."

Dean felt a big, goofy smile spread across his face. "You could say that." He shifted in his seat, just to feel the lingering soreness in his backside.

"So."

"So?"

"So, you gonna show me?"

He gaped at her. "*Show* you?"

"Show me the ghost video." She nudged his ankle with her foot. "Keep up, Dean."

"Oh. I thought..." He shook his head. "Never mind. Um, yeah. Okay." Setting down his coffee, he closed the overnight video from the kitchen and opened the thermal imaging video. "I need to watch through the whole thing, but I'll fast forward and show you the ghost part first."

"Cool."

Kerry scooted her chair closer. Dean advanced the video to where he thought the relevant part was and hit play. The screen showed a static rainbow swirl which it took Dean a few seconds to recognize as the wall of one of Blue Skye Inn's bathrooms.

"What's that?" Kerry asked, pointing at the screen.

"The wall."

"Why'd you video the wall?"

"I think that was when Sommer and I were...um, talking." Pushing away the memory of Sommer's brief but brain-melting kiss, he fast-forwarded the two of them out of the bathroom and into the hallway, then returned to normal play. "Okay, now we're going in the second-to-last guestroom, which used to be Sommer's mom's sewing room. This is where it happens."

Kerry leaned forward, intent on the video. She let out a little squeak when Sommer's form appeared like a person-shaped flame. "Wow, that's wild. No wonder these things are good for finding people in the dark. There's no way you could miss *that*."

"Yeah." He bumped Kerry's shoulder with his. "Now keep your eye on the air right next to Sommer. Watch what happens."

They fell silent, both staring at the computer screen. After a few seconds, the blue-gray form took shape to Sommer's left. Kerry gasped. "Oh, shit. Look at that."

"Just wait 'til you see the drawer fly open all by itself."

When it did, Kerry yipped in surprise and clutched at Dean's arm. "Oh my God, Dean."

Laughing, he patted Kerry's hand. "C'mon, Kerry, you already knew that was going to happen. Sommer and I told you and Ron all about it last night."

"Yeah, well, hearing about it and seeing it are two very different things." She shot him a wide-eyed glance. "Are y'all sure there wasn't anything in the drawer?"

Dean nodded. "Not even a dust bunny."

"Hm. Wonder why the thing, the ghost or whatever,

opened that drawer if it's empty?"

"Who knows? Maybe there used to be something in there at one time. Maybe the apparition thought it was still there."

Kerry shivered. "That's creepy and kind of sad."

"Why?"

"Why creepy or why sad?"

"Both."

"Creepy because of a ghost *thinking*. Sad because what if it was something important Sommer needed to know?"

Pausing the video, Dean turned to face Kerry. "So you think the apparition was trying to communicate with Sommer in particular?"

She shrugged. "Sommer's the one who sees it all the time. It just makes sense that it's trying to tell him something."

"Hm." Dean picked up his mug and took a sip. "And Sommer said none of his employees have seen anything unless he was with them, which totally supports your theory."

Kerry's expression turned solemn. "Sommer never saw that ghost upstairs before, did he?"

"No. Of course he said he normally doesn't go in that room."

"Yeah, but still. I wonder..."

"What?" Dean prodded when Kerry trailed off.

"I don't know. Just..." Her brow furrowed. "Okay,

maybe this is dumb, but what if the ghost is, like, taking things to the next level?"

"I don't understand."

Chewing her lip, she studied the paused video on the laptop screen for a moment. "Sommer's seen that thing in the kitchen lots of times, but he never followed it before the other day, right?"

"Right."

"And y'all didn't find anything in the woods."

"Right again."

"And now, all of a sudden, for the first time, this thing appears to Sommer upstairs and makes a drawer open." She leaned against the back of her chair, picked up her mug and balanced it on her protruding belly. "It's almost like since y'all didn't find whatever it wanted you to in the woods, it decided to try something else."

It made sense. All the hairs stood up on Dean's arms. "Sommer's arranging for me to talk to his employees who were working at Blue Skye when his parents still ran the place. I'll have to make sure to ask them specifically about that room. Especially the housekeeper. Maybe he'll know something that'll help us figure out who or what this thing might be, and what it wants."

"I hope so." Kerry lifted her mug, took a long swallow and set it on the table. "Can I help you review stuff?"

Dean smiled. "I already promised you and Ron you could. Would you rather watch video or listen to audio?"

She pursed her lips. "Which one's easier?"

He snickered. "Lazy."

"Am not." She kicked his shin with one sock-clad foot. "What I meant was, which one am I less likely to miss important stuff on?"

"I know, I know." He thought about it. "Probably audio. Believe it or not, it's really easy to lose focus on one of these videos when you're watching them for more than a few minutes at a time."

"Gotcha." She gave him an eager smile. "So, what do I do?"

To Dean's surprise, Kerry took to evidence review like the proverbial duck to water. She had an impressive ability to pick out sounds which didn't belong in the general background noise. Unfortunately, the couple of faint voices and myriad other things she found turned out on closer listen to be either the investigators themselves or the normal noises of an old house. The revelation disappointed her, but she perked up when Dean told her how common it was to make that mistake.

When she nudged him for about the tenth time, he stifled a sigh and steeled himself for another mundane thump, squeak or entirely human voice. He paused his video and turned to Kerry. "Okay, what—?" He stopped when he saw her ashen face and wide, shocked eyes. "Kerry, what is it?"

She shook her head. "I don't know. But it isn't us this time."

Taking the headphones from around Kerry's neck,

Dean put them on, reversed the audio tape a bit and hit play. He heard his own voice, telling Sommer to question the entity in the upstairs room, followed by Sommer's shaky whisper asking who the thing was and what it wanted. For a moment, nothing happened. Then, just before the rattle of the drawer opening, Dean heard it.

He stared at Kerry. "Oh shit."

She nodded. "No kidding."

His fingers trembling, Dean played it again. The voice wasn't himself, wasn't Kerry or Ron or Sommer, though the soft lilt reminded him of Sommer. He reversed and listened to those mournful words over and over, until he thought he'd hear it in his sleep.

"Sommer," the voice breathed, an aching melancholy sigh. *"Sommer...I'm here..."*

Chapter Nine

By the time Sommer finished listening to the audio clip for the fifth time, his face was gray and tremors shook his body. Worried, Dean took the recorder from Sommer's unresisting hand, pulled the headphones off his ears and stared into his glassy eyes. "Sommer? Are you all right?"

Sommer blinked and focused on Dean's face. "Yeah. I'm okay, just..." He drew a deep breath and let it out. "It's weird, is all. Hearing my name like that."

"I can imagine. It shook *me* up, and it wasn't even talking to me." He set the equipment on Sommer's kitchen table, where he and Sommer were sharing a bottle of Blue Skye Pinot Grigio while Dean went over the findings from Tuesday night's investigation. "Do you recognize the voice at all?"

A strange, guarded expression flashed through Sommer's eyes and was gone before Dean could properly grasp it. Sommer shook his head. "I don't think so. No."

He's lying. Dean wasn't sure what made him think that, but the feeling that Sommer wasn't being entirely truthful with him was strong. "You're sure?"

Sommer dropped his gaze to the table. "Yes. I'm sure."

An ugly feeling nibbled at the edges of Dean's mind. He forced himself to ignore it. Sommer wasn't the first client to feel the need to hide a personal connection to a haunting. Whatever his reason was for lying, Dean had to respect it. For now, at least. There was a time and place for trying to force the truth from someone, and this wasn't it.

"Has anything else happened since then?" Dean asked. "Any more ghost sightings, voices, anything at all?"

"No, nothing." Sommer quirked a wry half-smile at Dean. "I haven't been upstairs yet, though."

"I thought you were going to search that room, and the dresser in particular."

"I was. I will." Sommer picked up his glass and took a sip. "But Carol was the one who checked the guests in yesterday, and she put them in that room, so I didn't get a chance to look."

Dean stared at Sommer's hands cupped around the curve of his wineglass and tried without success to suppress the memory of Sommer's touch. "Um. We can go do it this afternoon. If you want."

"I suppose we could. The guests checked out this morning, and Rich has already cleaned the room, so we ought to be able to search without being interrupted." Sommer looked over at Dean, and his thoughtful expression turned wicked. "What're you thinking about?"

Those fucking beautiful hands doing evil, wonderful things to me. He shoved his overactive libido into a corner of his mind and padlocked it in. They could fuck later.

Right now, they needed to search the upstairs room, and Dean had to nail down a time to interview Sommer's staff.

Dean cleared his throat and forced himself to look innocent. "Just thinking about the investigation. I still need to talk to Rich and Cody, and really anyone else who'd be willing to talk to me. And I want your input about how the rest of the investigation should go, considering the apparition we saw and what we've found on the audio."

Sommer arched a skeptical brow, but nodded. "All right. Rich has already gone home for today, and Cody's off, but I've already spoken to both of them and they can meet with us tomorrow, if that's okay."

"That's perfect. What time?"

"I told them nine, does that work for you?"

Lifting his glass, Dean drew a mouthful of pale yellow wine, held it on his tongue for a moment and swallowed. "I don't know, I might not be able to get over here that early. Kerry's my ride, and she's so *not* a morning person."

Sommer slid to the edge of his chair, leaned over and nuzzled Dean's ear. "Actually, I was sort of hoping you'd already be here in the morning."

A giddy rush of desire swooped through Dean's insides. He let out a breathless laugh. "I can be. If you want."

"I want." Plucking Dean's wineglass from his hand, Sommer set both his and Dean's glasses side by side on the table. He laid a palm on Dean's cheek and peered into his eyes. "Do you?"

"You know I do." Dean reached up to frame Sommer's face in his hands. "Can we play with your toys again?"

The smile that spread across Sommer's face promised all sorts of sin. Tilting his head, he captured Dean's mouth in a demanding kiss. Dean surrendered with a happy sigh. He wished they could stay here all day, kissing at the kitchen table until afternoon faded into evening and the sun sank behind the trees in a crimson blaze. But there was work to do, and Ron and Kerry were coming over in a few hours for dinner before starting this evening's investigation.

He broke the kiss and leaned his forehead against Sommer's. "God, Sommer. Kissing you totally scrambles my brains."

Sommer laughed, fingers raking through Dean's hair. "Same here. It's so easy to forget about everything else when you're with me."

Dean's chest tightened. The look in Sommer's eyes made him want to chuck everything and spend the rest of his days in Sommer's bed, which was just plain scary. Not least because the idea was so damned attractive.

With a huge effort, Dean let go of Sommer and pushed to his feet. "Okay. Well. I'm ready to go search that room if you are."

"I'm ready." Rising to his feet, Sommer picked up his wineglass and drained it. "Should we bring your camera?"

"Oh, good idea. Hang on, I'll go get it."

He ran into the parlor and grabbed his camera and a flashlight from the coffee table. Sommer was waiting for him in the foyer. They climbed the stairs hand in hand and headed into the old sewing room.

A few minutes later, they'd opened and inspected every drawer in the dresser, shone the flashlight under it, even pulled the heavy old piece of furniture away from the wall to look behind it. The whole thing was as empty as the bottom right drawer. A thorough search of the rest of the room yielded the same result.

Sighing, Dean flopped onto his back on the braided rug. "Nothing. Not so much as a damn cracker crumb."

"Nope." Sommer stretched out on the floor beside Dean and stared thoughtfully at the white ceiling fan. "At least we know Rich is doing his job."

Dean laughed. "That's one way to look at it."

"Mm-hm." Rolling onto his side, Sommer propped himself on one elbow and gazed down at Dean. "We have a while before Ron and Kerry come over. What would you like to do?"

Dean pretended not to notice the way Sommer's voice went all soft and sultry. "Well, we have to make dinner."

"I'm just making eggplant parmesan, salad and bread. It won't take long." Sommer slid closer and leaned over Dean, one hand on his chest. "Stop pretending you don't know what I'm after. Kiss me."

The heavy look in Sommer's eyes made Dean's stomach flutter with anticipation. Grinning, he hooked an arm around Sommer's neck and pulled him into a kiss. Sommer's mouth opened, his tongue winding around Dean's.

Dean didn't break the kiss until Sommer lay clutched between his legs, their erections rubbing together through their jeans. He cradled Sommer's face in his hands and forced Sommer's mouth from his. Sommer let out a small noise of distress.

Dean gave him a dazed smile. "We're both gonna shoot in our pants if we keep this up. Want to go down to your bedroom?"

"I guess we should. Rich would kill me if we got spunk all over the rug." Stifling Dean's laughter with a swift, chaste kiss, Sommer wriggled free of the grip of Dean's legs and stood.

Dean took the hand Sommer offered and let himself be pulled to his feet. As they retrieved the flashlight and camera and walked to the door, he thought he felt a breath of icy air against his arm. He frowned. "Hey, Sommer?"

"Yeah?"

Dean was about to ask if Sommer had felt the brief cold, but something in Sommer's face stopped him. A tightness around Sommer's mouth, a flat gleam in his eyes.

He doesn't want to tell me. He felt it, maybe felt or saw something else too, but he doesn't want me to know.

Tamping down the automatic flash of hurt, Dean forced a smile. "Just wondering if I could help you cook dinner tonight."

Sommer's eyebrows went up. "Sure, if you want."

"I'd like to, yeah. I'm not very good, but I think it

could be fun to cook with you."

At least it was true, even if he hadn't planned on the conversation taking that particular turn. That adorable crooked smile lit Sommer's face, nearly making Dean forget all about cold spots and misty apparitions and whatever the hell Sommer wasn't telling him.

A hard chill clawed at his back as he followed Sommer into the hall. He ignored it. They had almost a month of investigation ahead of them. Plenty of time to solve the mystery of what was happening in this house, and figure out Sommer's connection to it. With any luck, Sommer would eventually come clean about recognizing the voice on the audio, and tell Dean why he'd kept that fact a secret.

Dean tried to tell himself it made no difference whether or not Sommer ever talked to him about it. It wouldn't affect the investigation much one way or another, really, so he shouldn't feel this unbearable yearning for Sommer to open up to him. It shouldn't matter this much.

It shouldn't. But it did. It *did*, and he had no idea what to do about it.

That night, the dresser drawer in the old sewing room opened by itself again. Dean missed it, since he'd partnered himself with Ron this time. Kerry was beside herself with excitement when she and Sommer came downstairs to report their experience. She was still talking about it when she and Ron left just after midnight. Sommer spent the rest of the night lost in thought. Dean eventually gave up trying to talk to him and dragged him off to bed, where he finally got Sommer's full attention.

Afterward, Dean lay staring up at the ceiling while Sommer slept beside him. He figured since he couldn't sleep through the noise of theories and suspicions whirling in his brain, he might as well try to work out just what was going on here.

Fact number one. Whatever entity haunted this place, it only manifested itself—whether through a physical form, a drawer opening or a cold touch—when Sommer was around. That much had become abundantly clear. Dean would have to ask the staff if they'd ever seen anything when Sommer wasn't with them, but he had no doubt anymore of what the answer would be.

Fact number two. So far, the apparition had only been seen in the kitchen and the upstairs guestroom. The old sewing room. In Dean's experience, when an intelligent haunt persistently appeared in a particular place, it had a reason. Spirits often manifested in the place where their bodies died, or in places that were important to them in life. Was that the case here? If so, why had this entity only now begun to appear in the upstairs room?

Of course, Dean didn't know for a fact that no one had seen the apparition upstairs, but he found it hard to believe that Sommer's employees—or guests, for that matter—would fail to mention seeing a ghost in that room.

Which brought him nicely to fact number three—this haunting was escalating. And Dean knew in his bones that the reason had something to do with the connection between Sommer and the upstairs room and that mournful voice whispering his name.

A yawn took Dean by surprise. He glanced at the clock and was shocked to see it was almost three a.m. Making a mental note to find out who had died in this house, and how, Dean rolled over to spoon himself against Sommer's bare back. He shut his eyes and pressed his forehead to the tangled hair at the back of Sommer's neck. Within a few minutes, he felt consciousness slipping away. He drifted off with the comforting rhythm of Sommer's heartbeat in his palm.

♥

"Yeah... Yeah, of course it's okay... No, no problem at all. We're not busy right now, we'll be fine... Okay... Okay... All right. Give your mom my condolences. Bye."

Dean looked up from his coffee as Sommer clicked the phone off. "What was that all about?"

"That was Rich." Sommer picked up his coffee mug from the counter and plopped into the chair next to Dean's. "His grandfather died last night. He's flying out to Sioux Falls this afternoon for the funeral."

"Oh my God." Dean took Sommer's hand, weaving their fingers together. "Were he and his grandfather close?"

"Not really, no. But there's a lot to sort out, so he's going to stay there for a couple of weeks and help his mom get everything settled." Sommer gave him a tiny smile. "I guess you won't get to talk to him any time soon, Dean. Sorry."

"Hey, no big deal. I just feel bad for Rich."

"You can still talk to Cody, if you like." Leaning back in his chair, Sommer peered at the clock. "He should be here any minute. I told him to come down to the house before going up to the winery today."

"Yeah, that'd be good." Dean scratched the stubble he hadn't yet shaved from his chin. "I should probably ask if there've been any paranormal-type incidents at the winery, or out in the vineyards."

"Nobody's mentioned anything to me, but it certainly wouldn't hurt to ask."

A loud knock rattled the glass in the kitchen door. Dean glanced up and saw a head of curly blond hair through the gap in the sheer cream-colored curtains. "That must be him now."

Sommer gave Dean's hand a quick squeeze before rising and crossing the room. He opened the door and stood aside. "Good morning, Cody. Come on in."

"Thanks, boss." Cody sauntered inside. He gave Dean a friendly smile. "Hi, you must be Dean." He stuck out his hand. "I'm Cody. Pleased to meet you."

Dean rose and shook the boy's hand. "We've actually met before. You waited on my friends and me when we came out for Karaoke Night on Saturday."

Not even a week. Such a short time to already feel so comfortable with Sommer. To feel like half of a couple.

Dean shook off the thought. It made him feel

141

dangerously warm inside.

Cody tilted his head sideways. "Oh, yeah, I remember. You were with Sommer's friends." He grinned, showing dimples. "Sorry, I don't have a very good memory for faces."

"No problem. I bet you meet so many people every day it's hard to keep them straight."

Sommer sidled up and wrapped a possessive arm around Dean's waist. "Well, Cody, I know you have to be at the winery in half an hour, so why don't we get started?"

Cody's blue eyes took on an amused glint. "Okay, sure." He pulled out a chair and plunked himself into it, shooting Dean a look that said he'd seen Sommer's jealous streak before. "What'd you want to ask?"

Settling in his chair, Dean picked up the audio recorder he'd brought. "First off, is it okay if I record you? If not, that's fine, I have a notebook, it's just that my handwriting kind of sucks and it's hard for me to read my own notes sometimes."

Cody laughed. "It's fine if you record me. I don't mind."

"Great." Dean clicked on the recorder. "So. Cody. You ever seen any ghosts here?"

"He didn't flirt with me at all," Dean said fifteen minutes later as Sommer shut the door behind Cody. "You said he would flirt."

Sommer grinned. "What, are you disappointed?"

"No." Dean grabbed Sommer's wrist as he approached and pulled him down for a kiss. "I *am* a little disappointed that he wasn't able to help any, though."

"I know, and I'm sorry."

"Don't be." Smiling, Dean touched Sommer's cheek as he straightened up. "I said he wasn't any help, but really he was, just not in the way I'd hoped. Knowing he *hasn't* experienced anything paranormal is actually helpful in its own way."

"I'm glad." Sommer walked over to the sink and began washing the dirty coffee mugs.

"Yeah. I think Rich is the one who's gonna be the most help, though."

Sommer shot a curious glance over his shoulder. "Why's that?"

A very good question. In fact, Dean had no idea why he was so sure Rich would know anything particularly useful. Rich was the only employee who'd been at this house on a regular basis since before Sommer's parents disappeared, but that didn't mean he would be able to shed any light on the case. Nevertheless, Dean was positive he could.

"Just a feeling." Rising to his feet, Dean crossed to where Sommer stood at the sink. He wound both arms around Sommer's waist and kissed his neck. "You know what?"

Sommer leaned into Dean's embrace with a soft hum of pleasure. "What?"

"I'm kind of glad Rich isn't here right now."

"Mmmm. Why?"

Grasping Sommer's shoulders, Dean turned him around. "Because if he was here, I couldn't do this."

He dropped to his knees, undid Sommer's jeans, pulled out his flaccid cock and swallowed it before Sommer could say a word. Above him, Sommer let out a surprised squeak. Wet, soapy hands dug into Dean's hair. Sommer's hips began to move, fucking Dean's mouth even before he was fully hard. Dean shut his eyes and let himself get lost in the taste of Sommer's skin and the smell of desire heavy in the air.

Kneeling at Sommer's feet, eyes closed and mouth full, Dean could admit to himself the real reason he was glad he'd have to wait two weeks to talk to Rich. The housekeeper was the key to solving the mystery of Sommer's ghost. Dean felt it in his bones. And once the case was solved, Dean had no reason to stay.

The thought of leaving, of never seeing Sommer again, made Dean feel cold and empty inside.

He concentrated on Sommer—the musky scent of his skin, the sharp taste of pre-come, the feel of Sommer's cock pistoning in and out of his throat. Whatever happened in the future, he had this, here and now, driving away the icy lump in his belly to make him feel warm and full again. He intended to enjoy it while it lasted.

Chapter Ten

After a few days of intending to go back home with Ron and Kerry and ending up spending the night with Sommer, Dean finally gave up and moved his things to the Blue Skye Inn. Kerry not only didn't argue, she encouraged it. According to her, he and Sommer had both been in need of—as she put it—"a good fuck or ten" for far too long and thus spending the next two or three weeks together would do them both a world of good.

Dean wasn't fooled by her casual acceptance of the situation. He'd seen that particular gleam in her eyes before, and he knew what it meant. She was a romantic at heart, for all her crude language and no-nonsense attitude, and she could smell love in the air from a hundred miles away.

Not that she was always right, because she wasn't. Especially in this case. Dean wasn't in love with Sommer. In lust, maybe. No, *definitely*. Sommer made him feel like a horny teenager again. And he liked Sommer. A lot. The man was smart, sweet, funny, and all-round great company. But what he felt for Sommer wasn't love. It was far too soon for that, no matter what Kerry thought.

Ron, on the other hand, was usually oblivious to the finer emotions in others. Which was why it was so disturbing when, precisely eleven days after Dean went to stay with Sommer, he expressed the opinion Kerry had only hinted at.

"You're falling for him," Ron declared around a mouthful of black bean burrito. "Don't try to deny it. I can tell. And you know if *I* can tell, anyone can."

Dean shot a nervous glance around the packed restaurant. Carrburrito's was unusually busy, even for a Friday afternoon, and he couldn't help feeling like everyone around them was listening in, even though he knew that was ridiculous. "C'mon, Ron. Sex and love aren't the same thing at all. He's hot, I'm hot, we're both horny. End of story."

"Uh-huh. You just keep telling yourself that." Picking up his glass, Ron drained the last of his iced tea. He pushed his chair back and stood. "I'm getting more tea, you want some?"

"No thanks, I still have plenty."

"'K." Ron glanced at his watch. "Kerry should be here any minute, I think I'll go ahead and order her lunch."

Dean scowled at the remains of his tomato and rice quesadilla as Ron made his way through the tables to the counter. He wished he could say with certainty that Ron and Kerry were reading too much into the situation with Sommer, but he couldn't. A small but growing part of him thought maybe they were right.

The sad thing was, he had no idea if his feelings for

Sommer really ran as deep as his friends believed, or if it only seemed that way because he wanted so desperately to love someone, and be loved in return.

He shook his head and sighed. *Sad, Dean. Very sad.*

"What're you sighing about?"

Dean started at the sound of Kerry's voice behind him. He turned in time to see her lower herself into the chair beside his. "Oh, hi Kerry. How'd everything go at the doctor's?"

"Fine." One hand rubbing her belly, she pinned Dean with an intent look. "So. What were you sighing about? And don't try to change the subject again."

"Nothing. Just thinking about the ghost, and wishing we could figure out just what the hell's going on." He gave her his best innocent look.

Her expression said she didn't believe him, but she didn't push the issue. "Are y'all still seeing and hearing things at the inn?"

"Every night."

She shuddered. "Creepy."

Dean nodded his agreement. The haunting had escalated to the point where the sight of the amorphous figure was almost commonplace. They saw it during every investigation. On the nights when Sommer had guests and they weren't able to investigate, cold spots and a feeling of being watched followed them into Sommer's bedroom. A couple of times, they'd even seen the apparition hovering just inside the bedroom doorway.

In the old sewing room upstairs, the atmosphere of

sorrow and deep regret had become so thick as to be nearly tangible. Sommer refused to go in there anymore, devastated by the weight of sadness that hit him every time he walked through the door. Dean felt it too, though it didn't affect him as much as it affected Sommer. Even the guests had noticed, to the point where Sommer had stopped renting out that room altogether.

The strangest thing of all was, the figure had stopped appearing in the kitchen. It only appeared in the guestroom now, and sometimes in Sommer's room. It was an unusual development, and Dean wasn't sure what to make of it. He'd never been involved in a case quite like this one. He felt as if he were groping in the dark toward a solution he sensed on a subconscious level but couldn't quite see.

Ron's return to the table jarred Dean out of his thoughts. Setting a laden tray in front of Kerry, Ron kissed her on the top of her head and sat across the table from her. "Hey, babe. I got you the *pescado asada*."

"Perfect, thanks." She picked up her fork and dug in. "Mmmm. This is awesome."

"So what'd the doctor say?" Ron asked, curling his fingers around his refilled glass.

"Everything's fine. The baby's healthy as a horse." She grinned. "Kicks like one too."

Dean laughed. "Okay, there's a mental picture I didn't need. A horse in your belly."

She arched an eyebrow at him. "You're kind of a nutball, aren't you?"

"And you're just now figuring this out?" Ron teased.

Kerry threw a tortilla chip at him, then turned back to Dean. "Are we investigating tonight?"

Dean shook his head. "Naw, Sommer has guests. Almost a full house, for once."

"Oh." Kerry dipped a chip into the little bowl of *salsa verde*, popped it into her mouth and crunched it up. "I'm glad he has that much business, but I'm kind of bummed we can't come over and play ghost hunters again tonight. I'm starting to get seriously curious about who this ghost is, and why it's so attached to Sommer."

"Me too." Ron reached over and stole a stray bit of fish from Kerry's plate. "I've been trying to think of who might've died there, but I can't come up with anything."

"Yeah, none of the staff I've talked to knows anything about anyone dying there." Dean picked up his last tortilla chip and nibbled at the edge. "I've been meaning to do some research on that, but I keep forgetting."

Ron gave him an evil grin. "Yeah, Sommer keeps you pretty well occupied, doesn't he?"

"I've been helping out around the inn," Dean protested over Kerry's giggles. "I'm sort of filling in for Rich until he gets back."

"Speaking of which, he ought to be back soon, right?" Kerry asked.

Dean nodded. "He's flying home tomorrow and coming back to work Sunday."

Kerry looked shocked. "Already? Couldn't Sommer have at least given him a day to get over the jet lag?"

"He tried to. He told Rich he could take up to another week off, but he flat refused. Said he wanted to come back to work." Dean shrugged. "The best part of that is, I'll actually get to interview him before I have to go back to Mobile, and see if there's ever been any paranormal-type happenings at the inn before Sommer took over."

"I bet there hasn't been," Ron said, his expression solemn. "All of it seems to revolve around Sommer."

"Yeah. Which means whoever died there must've been connected to him in some way." Kerry's eyes went wide. "Oh my God, you don't think it could be one of his parents, do you?"

In fact, that very idea had been worming to the surface of Dean's mind for a while now, and he thought maybe Sommer harbored the same suspicion. It would certainly explain the way Sommer clammed up every time Dean tried to broach the subject of the spirit's identity. However, he didn't feel comfortable confiding his hunch to Kerry and Ron just yet. Not when Sommer was still so clearly struggling to come to terms with the possibility.

"I don't think there's any evidence to point to that," Dean answered, truthfully enough. "Besides, wouldn't someone know if that had happened? The staff would definitely have known, and the obituary would've been in the papers."

Kerry's shoulders sagged in clear relief. "You're right."

"So who do you think it could be?" Ron wondered.

Dean shook his head. "I don't know. But, like I was saying before, I'm planning to do some research and see if there are any records of a death there, especially anyone even remotely related to Sommer."

"I can do that, if you want," Kerry offered. "The library's open on Saturday, I could go over there tomorrow morning and poke through the town's death records for you."

"That'd be great, if you're sure you don't mind."

"Not at all. I like playing Nancy Drew." She cut off a chunk of burrito with her fork and scooped it into her mouth.

"Cool, thanks." Picking up his bottle, Dean took a long swallow of cold root beer. "I'd better go. I promised Sommer I'd be home by three."

Ron glanced at his watch. "It's only two. Does it take that long to ride out to Sommer's place?"

"You rode a *bike* all the way from Blue Skye?" Kerry scrunched her nose. "You're crazy."

"Apparently." Dean pushed away from the table, stood and stretched. "And yes, Ron, it does take me that long. I'm slow."

Kerry snorted. "You're not slow, Ron just has those freaky-ass mile-long legs, so he can ride faster. An hour's about average for us normal people."

Laughing, Dean bent and gave Kerry a hug. "Thanks for the moral support. So, y'all are coming out for karaoke tomorrow night, aren't you?"

"Yep, we're planning on it," Ron confirmed. "We'll see you then."

"Yeah, see you."

Dean left with a final wave to his friends and walked out into the cool, sunny afternoon. It wasn't until he'd strapped on the borrowed helmet and straddled Sommer's bike that he realized what he'd said just moments ago in the restaurant.

Home, he'd said. *I promised Sommer I'd be home.*

"Home," he whispered, testing the feel of the word on his tongue. It felt good to attach that word to Sommer. It felt right.

But it *wasn't* right. In less than a week, he'd be on a plane headed back to Mobile. Back to his life. A life that didn't include Sommer.

God, I may never see him again.

A gnawing pain hit Dean square in the chest. He bent over the handlebars of the bike, trying to get control of the emotions roiling inside him.

When the ache faded, he straightened up, mounted the bike and pulled out into the road. With any luck, the afternoon traffic would keep him busy enough to drive away thoughts of losing the unexpected happiness he'd found.

Friday night and Saturday passed in a blur for Dean. He knew he was acting withdrawn and pensive, and he knew Kerry, Ron and especially Sommer were worried. But he couldn't help it. The specter of leaving Chapel Hill had nested itself deep in his chest, and nothing he did would make it go away.

By Sunday morning, Dean could barely summon the energy to talk to Rich. Solving the mystery of the Blue Skye Inn's melancholy ghost just didn't seem important compared with the fact that in four days, the ghost and the inn and Sommer would all be in Dean's past.

The thing that made Dean sit down in the parlor with Rich and ask his questions was Sommer himself. Sommer needed this thing resolved. He needed to know who haunted him, and why. Kerry's search for deaths in the house had proven fruitless. Rich was their last hope for an answer. Which meant that Dean was going through with the interview. The need to help Sommer superseded everything else, including his own apathy.

Parked in the chair where Sommer had fucked him not so long ago, Dean switched on the audio recorder and twisted around to face Rich, who sat on the love seat at right angles to Dean's chair. "Okay, Rich. First of all, have you ever seen or heard anything here that you'd describe as paranormal?"

Rich shook his head. "No."

"Have any guests or other staff told you about any experiences they might've had?"

"No." Rich ran a hand over his graying buzz cut. "Oh, well, Lisa saw the ghost that one time when she was in the kitchen with Sommer. Other than that, no."

"What about before Sommer arrived here? Did you ever see or hear of anything happening when Sommer's parents still ran the place?"

"No."

An unexpected question popped into Dean's head. He asked it before he could question his own instincts. "Were Sommer's parents...all right?"

Rich gave him a strange look. "All right how? They were nice people. A little weird, but nice. Good bosses."

"No, I mean were they...?" Dean scratched his chin, trying to think of a subtle way to ask. Unable to come up with anything, he decided to be blunt. "Would you have any reason to think either or both of them might be dead?"

The color drained from Rich's face. He glanced toward the archway into the hall. "Uh. I...I don't know."

"Sommer's not here," Dean said, guessing that Rich didn't want Sommer to hear what he had to say. "He's gone to get groceries. Whatever you tell me here is confidential." Dean hoped he wouldn't end up breaking that promise.

Rich stared at his hands clasped in his lap. "Sunny— that's Sommer's mom—was sick for a few months before they went missing. She never said anything to any of us, but you could tell she wasn't well. She lost a lot of weight, and her color was off. And she seemed exhausted all the time."

Dean's insides clenched. *God. Poor Sommer.* "So, do you think—?"

"I don't know." Rich looked up, dark eyes intent. "They had their own ways, you know? They never did things like other people."

Dean studied Rich's face, looking for answers. "What do you think happened to them?"

"Truthfully? I think they left. I think they went to find some private spot for Sunny to die." Rich shook his head. "I don't know if they ever told Sommer his mother was sick, but I bet they didn't."

The hard ache twisted Dean's stomach again. "And you never mentioned it to Sommer? None of you did?"

"It wasn't our place," Rich growled. "All we had was speculation. We had no business putting our shit on Sommer. He had enough to deal with."

"I know. I wasn't judging. Anyone would've done the same, I think."

Rich settled against the cushions with a grunt, evidently satisfied.

"Is there any way of finding out where they might've gone?" Dean asked. "An address book maybe? Anything?"

Shifting in his seat, Rich glanced at the archway again. "Uh, well, Sunny used to keep a journal. It would probably say something in there. But I don't know where it is. I mean, I know where she kept it, I saw her put it in there a couple of times, but I think it's gone now. Sommer should've found it when he cleaned his mom's things out, but if he did he didn't mention it."

A sudden idea sent Dean's pulse racing. If he was right... "Where did she keep the journal, Rich?"

"In the dresser in her sewing room. In the bottom right-hand drawer."

Chapter Eleven

In the end, Dean decided not to go looking for the diary on his own. He owed it to Sommer to tell him and let him decide what to do. If he wanted to go looking for his mother's journal, Dean would be right there beside him. If he'd rather believe it was gone for good, well, Dean would find a way to respect that.

He was sitting at the kitchen table, still working out how to approach Sommer with what he knew, when he heard the sound of Sommer's SUV on the gravel drive. Taking a deep breath, he stood and walked outside to help Sommer carry in the groceries.

Sommer had the back of the SUV open and was pulling out crammed-full plastic bags. Dean stood and watched him for a moment, admiring the taut curves of his ass in the snug faded jeans. Just looking at him made Dean's balls tighten.

Shaking off the urge to tackle Sommer to the ground and suck him off right there in the driveway, Dean walked over and laid a hand on Sommer's back. "Hey. Can I help with the groceries?"

"Hi, Dean." Sommer turned, six bags of groceries

hanging from his arms, and gave Dean a swift kiss. "Help would be great, thanks."

Dean hefted the rest of the bags out of the SUV, shut the door and followed Sommer into the kitchen. "Sommer, I—"

His words were cut off by Sommer's mouth on his. The kiss was deep and aggressive, and Dean's resolve to tell Sommer about the missing journal went flying right out the window. Dean's hands opened, the bags he carried clattering to the floor. He had a split second to hope the eggs weren't in one of those bags before Sommer's arms snaked around him to pull their bodies tight against one another.

By the time Sommer broke the kiss, Dean was painfully hard and his heart threatened to drum a hole right through his sternum. He stared into Sommer's eyes, feeling every bit as lust-drunk as Sommer looked.

"Take this," Sommer murmured against Dean's lips. He thrust a small, square something into Dean's palm. "Go into the bedroom. Undress and lie down on the bed, face up. Leave the box on the bedside table."

Dean swayed and grabbed at a nearby chair for support as Sommer drew away. "Uh. 'Kay." He managed a couple of staggering steps, stopped and frowned at Sommer, who'd started putting away the groceries. "Sommer?"

"I'll be there in a minute." Sommer shot him a smoldering glance. "I plan to keep you occupied for a while, so I need to get the groceries put away."

"I could help," Dean offered, though he wasn't at all sure he could even remember where everything went at the moment.

Sommer chuckled. "Go, Dean."

Dean's knees wobbled. Damn, but it was hot when Sommer ordered him around like that. He obediently turned and headed for the bedroom, the box Sommer had given him clutched in his hand.

The ceiling above him creaked, and he remembered with a jolt that one of the inn's guests for the night had already arrived.

What if he hears us? Dean wondered, putting the box on the bedside table and pulling off his long-sleeved T-shirt. *What if he hears me begging Sommer to fuck me harder? What if Lisa and Carol get here and they hear me too? Everyone'll know we're in here having sex. Everyone'll know he's fucking my ass so hard I won't even be able to sit down later.*

The idea was disturbingly exciting. Chewing his bottom lip, Dean kicked off his sneakers, wriggled out of his sweatpants and climbed onto the bed, lying on his back as he'd been told.

He didn't notice the door was not quite closed until he'd gotten settled. He was about to get up and close it when the stairs creaked out in the foyer. Dean froze, propped up on one elbow, and listened. Slow footsteps clomped across the hardwood floor. The front door opened and closed. Dean could hear Sommer putting away groceries in the kitchen, but the house was otherwise quiet.

Outside, an engine started up. A moment later, gravel crunched under tires. When the sound had faded away, Dean flopped onto his back, heart racing and breath coming short. He didn't know whether to be amused or irritated by how much interest his cock seemed to take in nearly being caught naked by a perfect stranger.

He almost jumped out of his skin when the door swung open. To his relief, it was just Sommer. "Sommer. Shit, you scared me."

"It's okay. The man who just left is the only one here right now other than us. No one else is scheduled to arrive until after five." He glanced at Dean's stiff prick and grinned. "Is that for me, or do you get off on exposing yourself to strangers?"

"It sounds so creepy when you say it like that."

"Oh, so that hard-on is for Mr. Davenport?"

"No way. This is totally for you." Spreading his legs, Dean cupped his balls in one hand and gave Sommer his best seductive stare. "So shut the door and get over here already."

Sommer's eyes went dark. He glided across the floor, his gaze fixed on Dean's face with such intensity that Dean wondered if a guy could come just from that *look*. "That's the last order you'll be giving me tonight."

"Okay," Dean breathed. His voice shook.

"Good." Stopping beside the bed, Sommer laid a hand on the inside of Dean's thigh. "I bought you something today. When I was out shopping."

Dean cut his gaze sideways to eye the innocuous little box on the bedside table. "You did?"

"I did." Sommer's palm slid up until his fingers brushed the sensitive skin behind Dean's balls. "Hand me the box."

Dean reached over, grabbed the box and put it in Sommer's outstretched hand. "What is it?"

Sommer didn't answer. Instead, he opened the box, plucked something out and held it up for Dean to see.

It looked like a silver armband, only far too small for anyone's arm. It was shaped like a slender snake, with a head that angled downward where the two ends overlapped and a tail that took a sharp upward curve. The tail ended in a slender ring. From the ring hung a short silver bar. When Sommer turned it a bit, Dean could see the bar was hollow.

At first Dean couldn't figure out what the thing was. Then it hit him, and his eyes went wide. He'd seen cock plugs before, but he'd never worn one. The mental image of hard steel around and inside his prick sent a violent shiver through him.

"Please don't feel like you have to wear it if you'd rather not," Sommer said, his voice soft and gentle. "But I'd like it very much if you would."

It took three tries before Dean could make his voice work. "Y-yes. I, I want to."

Sommer's smile melted away any lingering doubts in Dean's mind. He knew Sommer would never do anything to hurt him. If the plug felt anything less than glorious, all he had to do was say so and Sommer would put it away without another word.

Placing the jewelry back in its box, Sommer perched on the edge of the bed and rested the box on Dean's stomach. He opened the bedside drawer and pulled out a packet of lube. "Hold your cock up for me."

Dean curled shaking fingers around his shaft and held it upright. Sommer tore open the lube and propped it against the edge of the jewelry box, then lifted the silver snake from the box and slipped it halfway over the head of Dean's cock with a quick twist of his fingers. The feel of cold steel digging into his skin made Dean moan low in his throat.

The crooked smile Dean loved curved Sommer's lips. "Okay so far?"

"Yeah. Fine."

"Good." Picking up the lube, Sommer squeezed a dollop onto Dean's slit. His searching gaze met Dean's. "I'm going to put the plug in now, and get the band the rest of the way on. Tell me if you need to stop, all right?"

Unable to speak again, Dean nodded and gave Sommer a trembling smile.

Holding Dean's glans still with his left hand, Sommer swiveled the ring at the end of the snake's tail until the tip of the short plug rested against Dean's slit. "Here we go."

Hard metal pushed through the tiny opening, and Dean gasped. "Oh, fuck. Oh. Oh." The thing felt much larger than it was.

Sommer froze with the plug only halfway in and

stared into Dean's eyes. "Dean?"

"'M okay. Just...just wait a sec."

Sommer held still, his left thumb caressing the head of Dean's prick. Dean dug his free hand into the comforter and panted through open lips. He couldn't decide if the sensation setting his nerves on fire was more pain or pleasure.

A few seconds passed before the burn subsided and he decided it felt good. "More," he whispered. "All the way."

Sommer held Dean's gaze for a moment as if assessing his readiness before turning his attention back to Dean's cock. "Breathe, sweetheart."

Sweetheart. Dean's eyelids prickled. He drew a deep breath and blew it out. Sommer pushed, the metal band slid into place, then the steel plug was lodged inside Dean's cock and something about that made him feel whole for the first time in years.

Unclenching his left hand from the covers, Dean ran a wondering finger over the band around his prick. It fit snugly under the flare of the glans. He traced the gleaming snake from its sculpted head to its arched tail. When his fingertip brushed the edge of his slit where metal met skin, the touch sent a searing jolt up his shaft and into his spine. His body arched as if he'd been hit with an electric current. He'd never felt anything quite like it. And now, having felt it, he wasn't sure how he'd ever lived without it.

Gentle hands stroked his hair, his face, his throat. He

gazed up into Sommer's deep brown eyes, wishing his own would focus better. "S-Sommer. It's... Oh, my God."

"I know." Sommer bent and pressed a lingering kiss to Dean's lips. "It's almost too much, isn't it? Like burning alive, only it feels good."

Dean nodded. "Som. Mer. F-fuck...me. Fuck me. I n-need..."

Sommer's lips covered his again, soothing away his tongue-tied frustration. He buried his hands in Sommer's hair and kissed back with everything he had. If he didn't get Sommer's cock inside him soon, he thought he might die. His heart would explode from an overload of sexual urgency and he'd expire right there in Sommer's bed.

Ages later, Sommer drew out of Dean's arms. Dean grasped at him, whimpering when he moved out of reach. Sommer smiled. "I need to undress, beautiful. So I can fuck you."

Dean wasn't sure he understood all of what Sommer was saying, but he understood the fucking part. Summoning every ounce of patience he possessed, he clamped a hand around the base of his cock and watched with barely contained hunger as Sommer took off his clothes, rolled on a condom and climbed back onto the bed.

Naked, Sommer knelt between Dean's splayed legs, leaned over and retrieved the open lube packet from where it lay on the comforter. He squeezed the rest of the slippery fluid onto his fingers. "Legs up."

Dean grabbed the backs of his thighs, lifting his legs

up and apart. He let out a ragged moan when two of Sommer's slick fingers slid inside him. "Sommer. God, please."

"I know." Sommer's fingers withdrew, and the blunt head of his prick nudged against Dean's hole. "I love how you open up for me, sweetheart."

Dean's attempted answer morphed into a sharp cry when Sommer penetrated him. "Oooooh, oh yes. God."

"Mmmm." Sommer fell forward onto his elbows, bringing his face within kissing distance of Dean's. He thrust forward enough for his prick to nail Dean's gland and make him cry out again. "Dean..."

The aching need in Sommer's voice was nearly enough to bring Dean to the brink. Letting go of his thighs, Dean wrapped his legs around Sommer's waist and splayed both hands on either side of Sommer's face. "Sommer. Fuck me."

With a soft groan, Sommer began to move, rocking his hips in a slow, steady rhythm. Dean tugged his face down, and their mouths locked together.

Between his own moans and grunts and whimpers, Dean heard the kitchen door open, heard footsteps and the voices of Carol and Lisa arriving for work. He knew they'd hear him if they came up the hall to the front of the house, but he didn't care. He was lost in an overwhelming barrage of sensation, and nothing else mattered. Sommer's cock pounded his ass in an increasingly frantic pace, Sommer's warm breath panted against his lips as the kiss broke. The rub and press of their bare bellies against Dean's trapped cock jarred the plug and made his whole body sizzle, and God, how had he ever existed before this?

Too soon, Dean felt his orgasm blossoming inside him. Tingling heat spread from his cock to his ass, down his thighs and up his spine. For a second everything went still and breathless. He could hear his pulse in his skull, could count the beads of sweat on Sommer's brow. Sommer's cock plunged deep to nail his gland, and Dean came with a keening wail. His vision went gray with the force of it, all sound fading into white noise.

Dean's eyelids drooped and closed. When he opened them again, Sommer lay propped up beside him, watching him with something close to panic. "What's wrong?" Dean whispered, reaching out to touch Sommer's cheek. "Are you okay?"

Sommer laughed, the sound high and wild with obvious relief. "Me? I should be asking *you* that."

"How come?" Dean frowned. "Wait, when did you...?" He trailed off, thinking as hard as he could with his brain still half shorted out. The last thing he remembered was coming. Sommer had still been inside him then, approaching his own release. Clearly that had already happened, but Dean couldn't remember it.

"You passed out." Sommer gave him an anemic smile. "Right when I came, I might add, which was pretty terrifying."

Dean winced. "Oh, shit. Sorry."

"I hardly think you had any control over it." Sommer

ran a thumb along the line of Dean's jaw. "It was only for a few seconds, but I really think you ought to just stay in bed for a while."

"No, there's no need for that." Dean tried to sit up. Sommer's hand on his chest held him down. "Sommer, come on. I'm okay, really."

"Maybe. Probably. But I'd never forgive myself if you weren't, and something happened to you." He pressed two fingers to Dean's lips, stopping his protest before it started. "Humor me, okay?"

How any sane human being could possibly resist those big brown puppy-dog eyes, Dean had no idea. He sure as hell couldn't. With a resigned sigh, he relaxed back onto the pillows. "Okay. But I'm going to pretend I'm your kept boy, and I'm waiting naked in your bed because that's what I'm supposed to do."

Sommer arched an eyebrow at him. "Who says you're only pretending?"

Dean knew Sommer was teasing, but the idea started a simmering fire in his gut. He flashed the evil grin that always made Sommer's cheeks flush. "All right, Master. I'll be right here, naked as a jaybird and ready to serve you."

The growl Sommer let out made Dean's spent prick twitch, jostling the plug and sending hot and cold waves rippling through him. *Christ on a crutch, you sure can't forget it's there.*

Not that he wanted to. He liked it there, and not just because of how it felt.

Burying a hand in Dean's hair, Sommer bent until his lips brushed Dean's. "Leave that cock plug in. To remind you of who you belong to."

Warmth bubbled up in Dean's chest. Smiling, he grasped the back of Sommer's neck and kissed him. Sommer opened to him with a contented hum.

Never in a million years would Dean have thought he'd actually like the idea of belonging to someone. He'd always been something of a free spirit. Even with Sharon, he'd never thought of himself as being *hers*. But the fact was, with Sommer, he liked it. Loved it, in fact. Reveled in the thought of belonging heart, body and soul to Sommer. It didn't matter that they were playing a temporary game, and that this would all go away in a few days. Dean wanted it to be real. Wanted it so badly it hurt like a toothache. And how many kinds of wrong was that?

Eventually Sommer broke the kiss and drew back. "I need to go. My other guests will be here soon, and Lisa will need help with dinner." His dark eyes studied Dean's face with transparent worry. "Will you be all right alone?"

Dean smiled. "What, lazing around in bed? I'm pretty sure I can handle that without croaking."

Laughing, Sommer kissed the end of Dean's nose. "Well, I guess if you're up to being your usual smart-ass self, you'll be okay." He pulled away from Dean's arms, slid to the edge of the bed and stood. "But you're under strict orders to stay right here, okay?"

Dean gave him a mock-serious salute. "Yessir."

Sommer shook his head, but his eyes sparkled. He

bent down and came back up with his jeans in his hand. "I'll bring you dinner in bed," he said, pulling his pants on. "And if you're very, very good and don't move from this bed before I tell you to, I'll let you play with your favorite toy later."

The promise of having Mr. T—as he'd dubbed Sommer's ridged, vibrating black dildo—up his ass again made Dean's hole clench in gleeful anticipation. "You got it, Boss." A thought struck him, and he frowned. "Um, can I pee with this cock plug in?"

"You came, didn't you?" Sommer swiped his sweater off the floor and pulled it on.

Dean blinked. "Yeah. I guess I did."

Chuckling, Sommer took Dean's prick in one hand, held the head toward Dean and pointed at the plug. "It's hollow, so you can leave it in for long periods of time."

Dean swallowed against the rush of sexual excitement that swooped through him in spite of his recently sated state. "Oh. I see."

A slow smile spread across Sommer's face. "You really like having that plug inside your cock, don't you?"

Dean nodded, never once looking away from Sommer's eyes. "I do, yeah." *Mostly because it means I'm yours.*

He kept that part to himself.

"Okay, I'm going to work now." Sommer leaned over, a hand on the mattress on either side of Dean's head. "I'll check in on you in a little while, okay?"

"Sure." Dean tilted his face to accept Sommer's kiss.

"I'll be right here."

Sommer slipped on his shoes, walked across the room and opened the door. As he started into the hall, he turned, and his gaze caught Dean's. For a long moment, they stared at each other, a universe of things unsaid hovering between them. Then Sommer looked away, and the sense of something momentous about to happen evaporated.

Stepping out into the hall, Sommer shut the door. The floorboards creaked under his feet as he walked down the hallway to the kitchen.

Dean lay gazing up at the ceiling, listening to the sounds of people bustling around the house. He really should use this opportunity to think about Sommer, and what exactly was happening between them. They didn't have much time left together. Whatever they were to each other, Dean knew he had to figure it out and come to terms with it before he left, or it would haunt him. But he was so tired, and Sommer's bed was so deliciously soft.

"I can think about it later," Dean mumbled to himself. Closing his eyes, he let himself drift to sleep.

Dean woke to a dull red light on his face. He pushed to a sitting position and glanced around. He was alone in the room, though he could hear voices and the clink of dishes floating from the kitchen. The curtains still hung halfway open, and the setting sun shone through the crimson sheers which were drawn across the window. He glanced at the clock, and was surprised to discover that he'd only been asleep a couple of hours. He felt as invigorated as if he'd slept for a week.

Yawning, he scooted to the edge of the mattress and pushed to his feet. Electricity zinged over the head of his cock with the movement. The sensation wasn't as intense as it had been before, but there was no way he could forget the plug was there. The slightest sway of his prick, the faintest touch to the skin at the head, reminded him. Forcefully.

He grinned. Wearing clothes was going to be an adventure now.

Shuffling into the bathroom, he lifted the toilet seat and got a tentative grip on his cock. He decided that if peeing hurt, he'd have to remove the silver snake, no matter how much he wanted to leave it on. In. Whatever. Luckily, it wasn't an issue. There was a faint burn, so brief he barely felt it, then nothing. He shook himself off, washed his hands and headed back into the bedroom, deliberately making his cock sway more than usual just so he could feel the tiny shockwaves shooting up his shaft.

He was about to climb back into bed to await his personally Sommer-catered dinner, when he spotted the audio recorder he'd used for Rich's interview sitting on top of the dresser. He frowned. It had still been on the kitchen table when he and Sommer came into the bedroom, which meant Sommer must've found it and brought it in here.

It took Dean a moment to notice the headphones attached to the device. His stomach turned over when the implications hit him.

Sommer had listened to the recorder. Which meant he'd heard what Rich said about his mother. Which in turn meant he knew about the missing diary. And if he'd come to the same conclusion Dean had, as he almost certainly would...

Dean snatched his sweatpants off the floor and yanked them on, ignoring the spike of pleasure-pain that shot through him when the waistband caught on the cock plug. Sommer was going to need him when he found his mother's diary.

Chapter Twelve

Dean pulled his shirt on, then opened the bedroom door and padded barefoot into the hallway. He followed the hum of voices and the mouthwatering scent of roast beef into the kitchen.

Lisa looked up and smiled as he walked in. "Hi, Dean. I didn't know you were here."

"You must be deaf, then," Carol declared, hurrying in from the dining room and hefting a platter of pot roast from the counter. She grinned. "Have a nice nap?"

He managed a smirk in the interest of keeping the two women from suspecting anything might be wrong. "Very nice, thanks." He glanced around. "Where's Sommer? I need to ask him something," he added when he saw the teasing spark in Carol's eyes.

"He went upstairs." Lisa scooped the last of the buttery mashed potatoes into a huge bowl and turned to face Dean. "He ought to be back down soon. You joining us for dinner? You're welcome to eat with Carol, Sommer and me in here or with the guests in the dining room."

"I'm not hungry right now, but I'll probably grab some later. It smells great." He smiled, doing his best to keep his face relaxed. "See y'all later."

Both women headed into the dining room, arms laden with food. Dean waited until he was out of sight before breaking into a run. He took the stairs two at a time, jogged down the upstairs hallway and skidded to a stop in front of the closed door of the old sewing room. Drawing a deep breath, he turned the knob and pushed the door open.

Sommer sat on the edge of the bed, a small book with pale blue pages open on his lap. Dean moved forward, sat beside Sommer and rested a hand on his arm.

He didn't ask what the book was. He knew, and Sommer knew he knew.

"You found your mom's diary," Dean said, watching Sommer's face.

Sommer nodded. "It was *under* the drawer. The one place we never looked. It must've fallen behind the drawer when I opened it to clean it out."

"Probably so."

Sommer lifted his face to meet Dean's gaze. The stricken look in his eyes made Dean's chest constrict. "She found out she had cancer. She'd known it for months, and she didn't tell me. *Neither* of them ever told me. Why? How could they leave me in the dark about something like this?"

"I don't know. I wish I did." Shifting closer, Dean wound an arm around Sommer's shoulders. "I'm sorry."

Sommer gave him a wan smile. "I guess I should look on the bright side of things."

"The bright side?"

"Yeah." Sommer spread one hand over the words scrawled across the page. "The last thing my mother wrote in here was that she and Dad were thinking about going to some natural healing center up in Vermont. This is the first lead I've ever had on where to find them."

Oh God. He thinks his mother's still alive. Dread coiled in the pit of Dean's stomach. "So, you think that's where they disappeared to? Vermont?"

"Well, it's a place to start looking, at least, which is more than I had before." Sommer frowned. "You have a really strange look on your face right now, Dean. What are you thinking about?"

Dean stared into Sommer's eyes, frozen with indecision. Should he tell Sommer he believed his mother was dead? Or should he give in to the heartbreaking hope in Sommer's face and tell him what he wanted to hear? After all, Dean had no way of knowing for sure if Sunny Skye was dead. For all he knew, Sommer was right, and his parents had simply gone to New England in pursuit of a cure for his mother's cancer.

The problem was, Dean didn't believe that. His gut told him the sorrowful spirit haunting the Blue Skye Inn was indeed Sunny Skye. It explained everything, from the dresser drawer to the fact that the apparition never manifested unless Sommer was around. Not to mention the disembodied voice whispering Sommer's name with such longing.

You can't lie to him. It's cruel. He'd see right through it anyway.

Dean almost smiled at that. He'd always been an expert liar, when he wanted to be. Sommer was the only person he'd not only never been able to fool, but never really wanted to.

Shutting the journal, Sommer set it aside and rested a warm palm on Dean's cheek. "Dean. You're starting to scare me here. Please tell me what you're thinking."

Dean drew a steadying breath. "Sommer, I think...I think maybe your parents didn't go to Vermont."

Sommer's forehead creased. "What do you mean?"

"What I mean is... Well..." Dean sighed. God, this was hard. "Sommer, don't you think it's possible that...well, that your mother died here?"

Sommer blanched. "No, I don't. They went to Vermont. Mom's diary said they were planning to."

"She said they were *thinking* about it. There's nothing that says they actually planned it."

"How do you know?" Sommer spat, dropping his hand from Dean's face. He shook Dean's arm off his shoulders. "You haven't read it."

Dean forced back the surge of anger and hurt. Sommer was just lashing out, as anyone would do when confronted with something they didn't want to hear. "No, I haven't. I'm just going by what you said, which was that they were thinking of going to Vermont. Does the diary say if they actually made those plans?"

Sommer didn't answer, but the way he flushed and looked at the floor said enough.

Turning sideways, Dean took one of Sommer's hands in both of his. "I'm not saying this to hurt you, Sommer. It's just that everything here points to it. This spirit only appeared after you arrived, and it's only ever manifested when you're in the room. And it opened that drawer, over and over again. It's been trying to lead you there all this time."

"That doesn't mean anything. All it means is that the spirit, *whoever* it is, knew my mother would want me to find her journal, so I'd know what happened to her. That's all." Sommer shot a half-angry, half-pleading glance at Dean. "My mother had lots of friends, and not all of them are still alive. And she believed in life after death, and in ghosts. This spirit might even be a ghost she made friends with or something. Just because no one else ever saw it doesn't mean it wasn't here all along."

Dean didn't bother pointing out that entities inhabiting the twilight world between life and death didn't—*couldn't*—make friends with the living. Sommer was clearly in no state to hear it, and it didn't make any difference anyway. "I'm not saying I'm definitely right. Maybe I'm totally off base. But I don't think I am, and I can't lie to you about that. It wouldn't be right."

Sommer tore his hand from Dean's grip and bounded to his feet. "Shut up."

Dean stared up at him in shock. "Sommer, I didn't mean—"

"What, you think you have some sort of right to involve yourself in my personal business, just because we're sleeping together?" Sommer laughed, and the sound was hard and cold enough to freeze Dean's blood. "Just because you're a decent fuck doesn't give you the right to say *anything* about this. Just stay the fuck out of it."

That hurt. Dean shut his eyes and curled around the ripping pain in his chest. When he thought he could move without falling apart, he opened his eyes, pushed to his feet and walked out of the room. He didn't dare look at Sommer. If he had to see the contempt in Sommer's eyes right then, he'd shatter.

He walked downstairs as fast as he could on shaking legs and went into Sommer's room. It only took a few minutes to throw his things into his bag and pull on his sneakers. Hefting his bag onto his shoulder, he left the house and started walking down the long drive in the dusk.

What hurt worse than anything else was that Sommer never once tried to stop him.

When he reached the main road, he set his bag on the ground, fished out his cell and dialed Kerry and Ron's house. Ron picked up on the third ring. "Hello."

"Ron? Hi, it's Dean."

"Hey, man. What's up?"

"Um, I...I kind of need a ride. Could one of y'all come pick me up?"

"Sure. I thought you were at Sommer's, though."

"I am. Well, I'm standing by the road. We—" Dean broke off, choking on sudden tears.

A stunned silence followed. When Ron spoke again, his voice had gone soft with sympathy. "Hang tight, okay?

We're on the way."

"'Kay. Thanks."

"No problem. Love you, man."

Dean couldn't speak past the tightness in his throat, but Ron had already hung up anyway. Snapping his phone shut, Dean sat in the thin winter grass by the road to wait.

Alone in the gathering dark, Dean drew his knees to his chest, put his head down and let the tears come.

Chapter Thirteen

Dean narrowed his eyes at the paper in his hand. Tapping his pencil against his knee, he frantically wracked his brain for an answer. Nothing came to mind.

"Time!" Kerry called.

Damn. Scribbling the first word he thought of before Kerry noticed, Dean set the pencil down and clasped his hands over his paper. Ron glanced at him, and he flashed the blankly cheerful smile he'd been using ever since he'd left Sommer's place two days before. The worried crease between Ron's brows deepened.

"Okay, Dean," Kerry said. "You're first this time. 'Things that come from vending machines.'"

"Um. Okay." Dean scanned his sheet, and cringed. "I said 'bacon'."

Kerry's friend Morgan, sitting beside Dean on the sofa, snorted with laughter. "What the fuck? *Bacon?* How do you get bacon from a vending machine?"

"BLTs," Morgan's husband, Tom, suggested. "I got a BLT from a vending machine at the airport just last week."

Zoe, a pretty blonde from Ron's work, giggled. "That doesn't count, doofus."

Dean listened to the resulting argument with only half an ear. He couldn't care less if he got the point for "bacon" or not. He was sick of smiling and pretending to be happy. He wished the two other couples who'd come over to Kerry and Ron's house for dinner would go home, so he could mope like he wanted to. All he could think of was Sommer. Even Scattergories, normally his favorite game, couldn't hold his attention against his fantasies of what he'd do differently if he could live that fateful evening all over again. The thing was, he firmly believed he'd done right by telling Sommer the truth, so he wasn't sure what he'd change, exactly.

Maybe just the fact that I left, he thought, staring morosely at his paper. *You should've stayed, idiot. You should've waited until he'd settled down some, then tried to talk it out.*

Of course, the fact that Sommer hadn't come over or called or anything spoke volumes. Dean couldn't bring himself to beg for Sommer's attention, even if part of him ached to do just that.

He shifted in his seat. The cock plug he hadn't once taken off sent a shiver through him, and for a second he felt once again that wonderful sense of belonging. He wrapped it around him like a cloak.

"Okay, 'bacon' is officially allowed," Kerry announced, breaking Dean's reverie. "Morgan, it's your turn."

Before Morgan could give her answer, the phone rang.

Ron jumped up. "Y'all go ahead, I'll get it."

Dean watched Ron jog into the kitchen to pick up the phone. Beside him, Morgan gave her answer—bubblegum. He had to smile when Kerry let loose a string of colorful curses. That was the advantage to giving weird answers; yours weren't canceled out by someone else having the same one.

Ron appeared in the kitchen doorway, one hand over the phone's mouthpiece. "Dean, it's for you."

Dean's heartbeat stumbled, skipped and started galloping a mile a minute. Pushing to his feet, he hurried to where Ron stood. "Who is it?" He knew who he wanted it to be, but he didn't dare get his hopes up.

Ron gave him a cautious look. "Sommer."

Dean closed his eyes, drew a few deep breaths and opened his eyes again. "It's Sommer?"

"Yeah." With a quick glance at Kerry, Ron led Dean into the kitchen. "He sounds kind of freaked out, but he wouldn't tell me what's wrong. He said he had to talk to you first."

"Oh. Okay." Dean reached for the phone, his hands trembling.

Ron patted Dean's shoulder. "Take as much time as you need."

"Thanks." Waiting until Ron had left the room, Dean lifted the phone to his ear. His insides churned. "Hello?"

"Dean. Thank God. I was afraid you wouldn't want to talk to me."

Sommer's voice sounded high and shaky, as if he was on the edge of panic. Worried, Dean moved to the other side of the room to lean against the counter. "What's wrong?"

"I saw the ghost again, about two hours ago, in the kitchen this time. You know it hasn't appeared in the kitchen for a while now. I followed it, and...and I..." The sound of Sommer's breathing carried through the phone, rapid and harsh. "Can you come over here?"

"Sure," Dean answered, his mouth acting before his brain had time to think it over. "Sommer, are you okay? You're not hurt or anything, are you?"

"No. I'm fine."

He sounded far from fine, but Dean didn't think Sommer would appreciate him saying so. He chewed his thumbnail, thinking hard about what to do. He was torn. On the one hand, Sommer obviously needed him, and every cell in his body screamed to respond to that need. On the other hand, he was still bleeding inside from the wounds left by Sommer's last words to him, and he didn't know if he could take it again.

"I...I don't blame you if you don't want to come," Sommer quavered finally, breaking the heavy silence. "I said some horrible things to you, and I'm so damn sorry about that. I wish I could take it all back. You were..." Sommer's voice broke. "I know I don't have any right to ask this of you, but I, I really need you to come, Dean, please?"

Something about the tone of Sommer's voice set off

warning bells in Dean's head.

Don't ask. Just don't. He'll tell you off again.

But he couldn't not ask. Cursing himself for a masochistic idiot, he forced the words out before he could change his mind. "Sommer, don't take this the wrong way, but this doesn't involve anything illegal, does it?"

Silence. Dean's skin prickled.

Just as Dean was becoming seriously alarmed, Sommer spoke up in a shaking, barely audible voice. "I didn't do this. I don't know who did. But I think it's her, Dean, I think it's her, and I don't know what to do. Please help me."

A hard chill raised the hairs on Dean's arms, but there was no question of what he would do. Especially since he could make a pretty good guess about who "she" was. "Okay. I'm on my way. Where are you?"

"Outside the house. I didn't want my guests to hear." Sommer paused, and Dean swore he could feel the man's fear coming through the phone. "Thank you."

The connection broke. Dean pulled the phone away from his ear and stared at it, as if he expected to see Sommer's face in the earpiece. Returning the receiver to the cradle, he went to the kitchen door and beckoned to Ron. His friend excused himself and trotted over to where Dean stood.

"What's wrong?" Ron asked, following Dean around the corner into the kitchen.

"I'm not sure exactly. He wouldn't tell me either." Sighing, Dean ran a hand over his face. "It has something to do with the ghost, that's all I know. He wants me to come over."

Ron's brow furrowed. "Look, Dean, you never said what happened with you and Sommer, and I didn't like to ask, but..." Leaning closer, Ron laid a hand on Dean's shoulder. "You were really upset the other night. Are you sure you're okay to go over there?"

"No. But I'm going anyway." Dean gave his friend a wry smile. "You should've heard him, Ron. He needs me there, and goddamn if I'm strong enough to tell him no."

Ron studied his face for a moment, then nodded. "Okay. I'll go with you."

"Thanks, but I kind of think it would be better if I go alone."

"Are you sure?"

"Yeah." Glancing toward the doorway into the living room where the rest of the group was still playing Scattergories, Dean leaned closer and dropped his voice to a near-whisper. "I don't know what he found, Ron, but I think he's afraid he's going to be in some kind of trouble with the law."

"Oh." Ron frowned and scratched his beard. "Sommer would never do anything illegal."

"I know. But he's scared. He didn't specifically say he wanted me to come alone, but I got the idea that's what he wanted." Dean laid a hand on Ron's arm. "Can I use your car? I'll check out the situation and let y'all know what's up."

In answer, Ron crossed to the small table by the back

door, took the car keys from the drawer and handed them to Dean. "Call as soon as you can, and let us know you're both okay."

"Sure thing." Moved by a sudden burst of affection for his old friend, Dean flung his arms around Ron and hugged him hard. "Thanks. You're the best."

Ron patted Dean on the back as they drew apart, then went back into the living room. As he took his jacket off the hook beside the door and shrugged it on, Dean heard Ron's voice, followed by Kerry's. She sounded upset. Dreading a confrontation with Kerry, Dean hurried out the door. She didn't know the details of his falling out with Sommer, but he hadn't been able to hide how hurt he'd been, and Kerry had reacted accordingly. If Ron was telling her about Sommer's call right now, Dean didn't want to be around to hear Kerry rip Sommer to shreds.

He wasn't sure what it meant that he was so willing to run to Sommer's side after the things Sommer had said. Or maybe he *was* sure and just didn't want to think about it. Either way, he was going, because Sommer wanted him to.

Unlocking Ron's car, Dean slid into the driver's seat, started the engine and drove off into the night.

A Hummer, a battered red minivan, and an expensive-looking road bike were parked in front of the Blue Skye Inn when Dean arrived. He glanced at the upstairs windows. All the lights were off.

Dean was relieved. It was only ten-thirty p.m., and

he'd been afraid some of Sommer's guests would still be up. Apparently they were all asleep, which was good. Whatever had shaken Sommer so badly, Dean had a feeling it was something he wouldn't want the guests to know about.

"Sommer?" Dean called softly as he stepped out of the car. The front yard was shrouded in deep shadow from the trees surrounding the house, and Dean couldn't see a thing.

"Over here."

Dean turned toward the sound of Sommer's voice. Beneath the big oak, he could just make out the pale blur of a face. A creak of chains told him Sommer was sitting in the old swing.

Crossing the yard, Dean sat beside Sommer. "I'm here, Sommer."

Sommer turned to look at him. His brown eyes glittered in a stray beam of moonlight, the corner of his mouth hitching into a sad little smile. "Thanks for coming. I...I was afraid you wouldn't. Not that I'd blame you."

"We can talk about that later." Dean laid a hand on Sommer's knee. "Tell me what happened."

"I found something," Sommer whispered, staring into Dean's eyes. "Right at the spot that apparition led us to before."

Apprehension coiled in Dean's gut. "What did you find?"

Sommer stared into the distance. His fingers twisted

together. "A body."

Jesus. Swallowing against his suddenly pounding pulse, Dean forced himself to speak calmly. "Sommer, if you've found a body you'll need to call the police."

"I know. I know, just..." Sommer licked his lips, rocking in place. "They're going to think I did it, and I didn't." He turned and gave Dean a pleading look. "Just come out there with me, and look at it. Help me figure out what to do."

Dean knew he should persuade Sommer to go inside and call the police right away. But the terror and sorrow in Sommer's eyes undid him. Taking Sommer's hand in his, he squeezed gently.

"Okay. I'll go take a look."

Sommer's grateful smile made Dean's chest hurt. Keeping Dean's hand clutched in his, Sommer pushed to his feet. Dean rose alongside him. Leaning down, Sommer picked up a large flashlight which had been lying on the ground beside the swing. He switched it on and led the way toward the woods.

They walked in silence, fingers still wound together. The flashlight's wide beam glittered in the frost coating the grass. Sommer seemed calm, but his eyes were a bit too wide, his breath coming too fast. Finding a body behind his house would certainly explain that reaction, but it was more than that. The shock in Sommer's eyes seemed personal. Dean thought he knew why.

When they entered the stand of trees, Sommer's fingers tightened around Dean's. Sommer slowed as they approached the little clearing. "It's in there," Sommer said, aiming the flashlight at a pile of loose dirt surrounding a wide hole in the ground. The beam shook.

Taking the flashlight from Sommer, Dean walked over and knelt on the edge of the opening. Sommer went with him, his hand clutching Dean's in a painfully hard grip. The interior of the hole was shrouded in shadow. Steeling himself for whatever he'd see, Dean shone the beam inside the shallow opening.

"Oh, my God," Dean breathed, staring at the pile of white bones gleaming in the light. "Sommer, how did you find this?"

"I followed the ghost, like I told you. It came straight here, like before, and just hovered. I got the urge to touch it, and..." Sommer made a soft, strangled sound in the back of his throat. "It was cold. Freezing cold. But this time when I touched it, I felt *warm* inside. And I got this clear idea in my head, telling me to dig right here. So I went back to the house, got my shovel and started digging."

"It sounds like we've found your m—um, your ghost's body." Dean stared at the skull still half-buried in the dirt. The empty eye sockets stared back at him. He pressed his lips together to stop himself from pointing out what was, to him, painfully obvious.

"You were right, Dean."

To Dean's surprise, it wasn't even a struggle to avoid saying, "I told you so." He pressed his shoulder to Sommer's in a silent invitation for him to continue.

Sommer pointed into the excavation. "Do you see the ring on her finger?"

Dean leaned over to get a better look at the skeletal hand sticking out of the earth. An ornate Celtic knot ring shone silver on one bony finger. "I see it."

"I remember that ring. My great-grandfather made it himself, when he first emigrated here from Ireland. He gave it to the woman he married, and it's been passed down through the family ever since."

"Sommer..." Dean held Sommer's gaze, putting the question he couldn't bring himself to ask into his eyes.

The corner of Sommer's mouth lifted in a melancholy smile. "I think this is my mother."

Chapter Fourteen

By the time the police left, the eastern sky had begun to pale. Dean shut the door behind the last uniformed officer with a deep sigh and headed back into the kitchen. Sommer sat at the kitchen table, staring silently into the cup of coffee Dean had made him.

"Well, I guess that's it for now." Shuffling over to the table, Dean fell into the chair next to Sommer's. "I'll give Ron and Kerry another call in a little while. They don't need the car yet, since Ron's biking it to work, but they'll want to know what's going on."

Sommer nodded without looking up. "Were they upset when you talked to them earlier?"

Dean let out a rueful laugh. When he'd talked to them the previous night, Ron had taken the news with his usual laid-back calm. Kerry, predictably, had shifted gears from furious with Sommer to frantic with worry over him once she'd heard what happened. The only way Dean could talk her out of calling a cab to bring her straight over was to promise to call again after the police left.

"Not really," Dean answered. "They're worried about you, that's all."

"At least I'm not under suspicion yet." Curling his fingers around his coffee mug, Sommer lifted it and took a sip. "I don't mind having to stay in town. I wasn't planning to leave anyhow."

"They have no reason to suspect you. I heard one of the cops say it looked like the body had been there a long time. And that there was several years worth of weeds and stuff growing there." Dean didn't mention that he'd been deliberately trying to overhear the two officers' conversation, and he was pretty sure they hadn't meant for him to hear that bit.

Sommer glanced up, the barest hint of his normal sweet smile on his face. "Thanks, Dean. For coming over, and for staying with me while the police were here. I really appreciate it."

"I just wish they would've let me stay with you while they talked to you." Scooting his chair closer, Dean rested an elbow on the table and propped his chin in his hand. "I'm sorry your guests all left."

Sommer shrugged. "Me too. Not that I blame them. Being woken up near midnight by a bunch of cops stomping around and not saying what's going on wouldn't make me want to stay here either."

"You were awfully nice to refund their money and find them rooms at other places."

"I owed them that much. They didn't expect this sort of thing when they booked the rooms." Sighing, Sommer set his mug down and rubbed both hands over his face. "God, I really didn't need this though. I'm already running in the red."

Not knowing what to say, Dean reached out to run a tentative finger over the back of Sommer's wrist. To his surprise, Sommer took his hand and pressed the open palm to his cheek, eyelids fluttering closed and lips parting. "God, I've missed you. I know it hasn't been that long, but it felt like forever."

Dean's breath hitched as a sudden desire flared to life in his belly. *Bad timing,* his good sense warned him, even as his thumb caressed the corner of Sommer's mouth. *He was just led by what is probably the ghost of his mother to what is most likely her skeletal remains, and he's just spent hours being grilled by the police. He's not going to want sex right now.*

Sommer's eyelids rose slowly, as if it was a great effort. The whites of his eyes were bloodshot. He yawned, his gaze going unfocused for a moment.

"Sommer, you're exhausted." Dean moved his hand up to rake through Sommer's hair. "Go get some sleep."

Shaking his head, Sommer rose to his feet and went to lean against the counter. "Can't right now. Rich'll be here any minute, I'll need to let him know what happened. And I need to call Lisa and tell her she doesn't have to come cook lunch. And I should probably help Rich clean the rooms."

Pushing away from the table, Dean stood and walked over to stand beside Sommer at the counter. "I'll stay and help you with all that and whatever else needs doing, okay?"

Sommer looked away. "You don't need to do that."

"It's no problem. I want to." A thought struck Dean. He crossed his arms. "Unless I'm overstepping my boundaries again."

Evidently Sommer understood the venom in Dean's voice, because before Dean knew quite what was happening he found himself with his back pressed against the counter, Sommer's mouth taking his in an aggressive kiss.

Dean gave himself up to it with a soft moan. God, he'd missed the way Sommer's kisses always made him feel like the world had stopped turning for a while.

When they drew apart, Sommer cupped Dean's face in his hands and stared hard into Dean's eyes. "You aren't overstepping anything. You never did. Those things I said were just me being stupid." He caressed the corners of Dean's mouth with his thumbs. "Are we okay, Dean?"

Dean felt no hesitation this time. He laid his hands over Sommer's. "Yeah. We're okay."

The smile he got in return almost made him forget that he would be flying back to Mobile the next day, and he wasn't sure anything would ever be okay again after that.

Dean rose slowly from a dead sleep to the sound of someone moving around in the next room. He cracked one eye open. He was lying on a large, squashy sofa upholstered in muted maroon and gold, with a round maroon throw pillow under his head and a fluffy white blanket tucked around him. A moment of confusion gave way to the realization that he'd fallen asleep in the parlor.

He sat up. "Sommer? Where are you?" He had a distinct memory of lying down on the couch for a nap, and that memory included Sommer being with him.

"In the kitchen," Sommer called. "I made some coffee, come on in."

"'Kay." Throwing the blanket off, Dean indulged in a luxurious stretch before wandering toward the kitchen.

Yawning, he thought of the previous night and morning with Sommer. It felt good to be back with Sommer, despite everything. Even talking to the police all night instead of sleeping then playing assistant housekeeper all morning was okay because he'd been with Sommer through it all. He hadn't realized how lost he'd felt without the man until he came back.

The knowledge that they only had the dwindling remains of this one day left to be together clawed at Dean's insides. He wished he could ignore it. The thought of leaving Sommer behind forever made him feel desolate.

It doesn't have to be that way, you know. You don't have to get on that plane tomorrow.

The increasingly bold voice in his head was wrong, of course. He *did* have to go. Tomorrow morning, he was going back home, and that was that. But right here, right now, he was with Sommer, and he intended to make the most of it.

Pushing the morose thoughts to the back of his mind, Dean leaned against the frame of the archway between the parlor and the kitchen and watched Sommer pour hot, fragrant coffee into two large mugs. "Hi."

Sommer glanced over at him, a bright smile lighting his face. "Hi. Sleep okay?"

Dean nodded, scratching the stubble on his chin. "Like a baby. That couch is pretty comfy." He peered out the kitchen window. The clouds which had rolled in earlier had opened up. Rain pounded the grass and trees and pinged off the roof of Sommer's SUV. "What time is it?"

"About four." Picking up the two mugs, Sommer carried them to the table and sat in one of the chairs. "Oh, I forgot to get the creamer out."

"'S okay, I know where it is." Shuffling over to the refrigerator, Dean took out the bottle of cinnamon creamer, went back to the table and plopped into the chair beside Sommer's. He opened the creamer and poured a generous helping into his mug. "So. I guess your mother's ghost was trying to lead you to her body, huh?"

"I think so, yeah. Her body, and her diary, so I'd know what happened to her." His mug clutched between his hands, Sommer gazed thoughtfully out the window into the wet gray afternoon. "I wish she'd come back. I'd like to see her again, now that I know. Even though she couldn't talk to me or anything. It would've been different, knowing it was her." Yawning again, Sommer closed his eyes and rubbed the lids with a thumb and forefinger.

"Totally." Dean lifted his own mug and took a sip. "Where do you think your dad is?"

Sommer shook his head. "I have no idea. Right now, I'm not even sure I want to know. Either he was here when Mom died and he never told me—never notified anyone, in fact, just buried her out there in the woods and took off—or he left her when she was sick. Either way, I'm pretty angry with him right now."

"I'm sorry, Sommer. I know this has got to be tough for you. I wish I could do more to help."

Sommer set his coffee down and pinned Dean with a piercing look. "You've helped, Dean. More than I can tell you."

The gratitude in Sommer's voice tugged at Dean's heart. He gazed deep into Sommer's eyes, unsure of what he was looking for, but desperate to find it anyway.

What he saw was hot desire, underlaid with something Dean was afraid to name, because it couldn't possibly be true.

Wanting to replace that tender look with pure lust, he put his coffee down, leaned forward and pressed his lips to Sommer's in an insistent kiss.

A hoarse groan tore from Sommer's throat. His hand came up to tangle in Dean's hair, tilting his head to deepen the kiss. Dean whimpered as Sommer's tongue forced his mouth wide open. He loved Sommer's sexual aggressiveness, so shockingly different from his otherwise soft-spoken, almost demure demeanor. Kissing Sommer felt as natural as breathing, and just as necessary. It scared Dean how much he already craved Sommer's touch.

Don't think about it. Just let him take what he needs, enjoy it, and don't think about it.

Easier said than done, maybe, but Dean was determined not to think about that either.

Dean let out a startled yip when the phone rang. Sommer grimaced. "Stay," he ordered, laying a palm over Dean's hammering heart. "I'll be right back."

Obediently keeping his seat, Dean watched Sommer cross the room, pick up the phone and say "hello" in a lust-rough voice. The outline of his erection was clearly visible through the snug, faded jeans.

Dean's mouth watered. He barely heard Sommer greet whoever was on the other end of the line.

"Yeah, Dean's still here," Sommer said, glancing at him with a sly smile. "He helped me out with some of my work, then we had a nice long nap to make up for being awake all night." Kerry's voice floated through the receiver, saying something Dean couldn't make out, and Sommer laughed. "Yes, we really did sleep, actually."

Dean eyed Sommer's crotch. His erection was too tempting for Dean to resist. Especially since he hadn't tasted that gorgeous cock in three whole days.

Wondering if Sommer would punish him for what he was about to do—and halfway hoping the answer was "yes"—Dean stood, sauntered across the room and dropped to his knees in front of Sommer. The man's soft gasp when Dean flipped open the button on his jeans and tugged down the zipper made Dean's stiffening cock throb.

"Oh. Um. No, I haven't heard anything else from the police," Sommer said into the phone, his voice trembling a little as Dean pulled his prick out and rubbed his cheek against the head. "But they only just left a few hours ago, so... No, I'm not...oh God...a suspect, but...uh...I'm not supposed to leave t-town." He moaned, back arching to push his hips forward. "No, they... *Shit...* They haven't identified the body. It takes a lot longer than... Yeah, I'll...I'll let y'all know when I...when I hear anything."

Keeping his eyes rolled up to see Sommer's face, Dean ran his tongue in slow circles around the head of Sommer's cock.

Sommer closed his eyes and leaned his head against the wall. His free hand clenched in Dean's hair. "Dean's...um...eating right now. Can I bring...uh...bring him home later tonight? I promise not to keep him too late."

Sommer pumped his hips, driving himself deep into Dean's throat. Dean relaxed and let Sommer fuck his mouth. Being taken like this, head held still in a firm grip while Sommer's thick cock plundered his mouth, excited him tremendously. He rolled Sommer's balls between his fingers, drawing the musky scent deep into his lungs every time Sommer pulled back enough for him to breathe.

Above him, Sommer panted out a promise to call Kerry if Dean was staying later than eight. Dean swallowed around Sommer's prick, making him yelp and twitch. There was a click as Sommer hung up the phone, then a sharp tug on Dean's hair, yanking his head back. He stared up into Sommer's eyes, licking his lips.

"Get up," Sommer growled. "Take your clothes off."

Dean hurried to obey. Rising to his feet, he ripped his sweater over his head and tossed it aside, then reached down to pull off his shoes and socks. The jeans and underwear came off next, and Dean stood stark naked under Sommer's burning gaze. The wooden floor felt cool under his bare feet. His nipples pebbled in the chill of the drafty old kitchen.

"Nice," Sommer whispered, staring at Dean's exposed cock. "You're still wearing the plug."

"Haven't taken it off." Dean rubbed his thumb over the curve of the snake's tail. "I like how it feels. And I especially like that it makes me think of you."

An indefinable expression fleeted through Sommer's eyes. Closing the distance between them, Sommer pulled Dean to him and took a soft, tender kiss. The tip of his tongue traced Dean's bottom lip in a languid caress before he drew away. "Bend over that chopping block behind you."

Dean's knees almost buckled. Shooting Sommer a wide-eyed look, Dean turned around to face the low wooden chopping block in the middle of the kitchen floor. It was wide and sturdy, perfect for fucking on. Stretching his body in a way he knew was enticing as hell, Dean bent over and rested his cheek on the scarred and stained wood. He arched his back and opened his thighs, presenting himself for Sommer's pleasure.

Cool palms slid up the backs of his thighs, smoothing over his ass and spreading his buttocks apart. Dean jerked and cried out when a warm, wet tongue lapped at his hole. "Oh God. Sommer..."

"Mmmm."

The tongue stiffened, probed and twisted, the tip worming itself inside Dean. Whimpering, he clutched the edges of the block in a white-knuckled grip. Sommer's tongue plunged deep into his ass, Sommer's fingers sliding down to toy with the steel rod in his prick. Pleasure thrummed through his blood, making his head spin.

"Uh. God," he gasped. "Fuck me."

Sommer's tongue slipped from his hole and was replaced by two fingers before Dean could protest. "Can't. I'm out of condoms."

Dean let out an undignified whimper. He rocked his hips backward, forcing Sommer's fingers deeper. "Please."

"I can't use my cock on you. Not without protection." Soft hair tickled Dean's back as Sommer leaned over him, mouthing the crests of his shoulder blades. "All I have is my hands."

Yeah. His sexy fucking hands. Even in his lust-addled state, the hinted possibilities in Sommer's words did not escape Dean's notice. Summoning every ounce of concentration he could, Dean managed to form a question.

"Have you fist fucked someone before?" Dean's words

came out in a breathless rush.

"Yes. The last man I was in a relationship with loved being fisted." Sommer's fingers twisted in Dean's ass, zinging over his gland and ripping a cry from his throat. "You?"

"Yeah. Been a long time, though." Dean moaned, hips swaying as Sommer's careful fingers massaged his gland. "Oh God. Not...not here."

"Mm. Right." Leaving two fingers lodged deep in Dean's ass, Sommer straightened up, wrapped his free arm around Dean's waist and pulled him to a standing position. "Bathroom first. We'll get you cleaned out."

Trembling, Dean twisted sideways, wound an arm around Sommer's waist and leaned against him. He let Sommer lead him down the hall, through the bedroom and into the big, bright bathroom. Sommer's fingers remained inside him, making him feel strangely safe.

The fingers only withdrew when Sommer nudged Dean onto hands and knees on the thick green bathmat. Dean whimpered his distress at the loss.

Sommer let out a soft laugh. "I need to get everything ready. Feel free to finger yourself."

Dean shook his head, preferring to savor the anticipation of waiting for Sommer's touch. Folding his arms on the mat, he rested his cheek on them and watched Sommer take an enema set, a tube of K-Y and several thick towels from the narrow closet beside the pedestal sink. From his vantage point at floor level, he couldn't see Sommer fill the enema bag, but he heard the splash of water as Sommer adjusted the temperature, followed by the hollow gurgle of liquid flowing into the bag.

"Okay. All set." Bag and tubing primed, Sommer knelt on the floor beside Dean. He nudged Dean's knees further apart, then spread a towel underneath him with his free hand. His brown eyes gazed into Dean's, solemn and serious. "Are you sure?"

Dean nodded, staring into Sommer's eyes. "Yes. I want this."

He couldn't have pinpointed why he wanted to do such a thing now, with this man, but he did. Over the past three and a half weeks, he'd come to feel more comfortable with Sommer than he ever had with anyone. Just being in Sommer's presence made him feel safe and cared for. He knew he could trust Sommer with this.

Sommer nodded. Bending down, he planted a kiss on Dean's cheek before moving out of his field of vision.

Dean heard the click of the lube cap opening. Cool, slick gel was smeared over his hole. His hum of pleasure turned into a soft gasp when the nozzle of the enema tubing slipped inside him.

"Tell me if you need to stop," Sommer said, the tremor in his voice giving away the extent of his excitement. "I'll go slow."

Dean moaned as the warm liquid slowly filled his rectum. He'd always enjoyed the sensation, but it had usually been a solitary activity since very few of his past lovers had been willing to share this experience with him.

It was, he reflected, far more enjoyable when someone else performed it for him. The level of intimacy was phenomenal, nearly as intense as the fisting to follow.

He was on the verge of telling Sommer to stop when the flow of water cut off. The nozzle was gently withdrawn from his ass.

"You're beautiful," Sommer whispered, one hand caressing Dean's hip, the other massaging his belly in soothing circles. "I love that you trust me enough to let me do this."

"God. Yes. Sommer. Your hands." The words came out broken and nearly incoherent, but Dean didn't care. He figured Sommer got the message.

They stayed like that, Dean on knees and chest on the bathmat with Sommer stroking his body and whispering endearments, until Dean couldn't wait any longer. He pushed up to a kneeling position, which Sommer seemed to understand immediately. Helping Dean to stand, Sommer led him to the toilet and headed into the bedroom.

Once again, Dean didn't have to say a word for Sommer to know what he needed. The moment he flushed and stood up, holding onto the nearby sink for support, Sommer came hurrying through the door to his side.

"Lean on me," Sommer murmured, slipping an arm around Dean's waist.

Dean washed his hands, then allowed Sommer to support him as they made their way into the bedroom. His legs felt rubbery, his head swimming with an intoxicating mix of relaxation and desire. His cock was still rock hard, oozing tiny drops of pre-come through the hole in the plug.

The heavy burgundy drapes had been pulled shut across the bedroom windows. The watery gray light leaking in around the edges did nothing to illuminate the room. A single lamp burned on the dresser, the burgundy shade throwing a muted light around the room.

The bed looked even more inviting than usual, with the thick comforter folded at the foot and fluffy white towels spread out over the sheets. Sommer helped Dean onto it, lowering him gently onto his back atop the layer of towels.

Leaning over, Sommer pressed a soft kiss to Dean's lips. His hands stroked Dean's hair, his face, the curve of his shoulder. When they drew apart, Sommer's eyes shone with such tenderness it brought a lump to Dean's throat.

Holding Dean's gaze, Sommer stood and began pulling his clothes off. Dean watched, fascinated by the way the lamplight glowed red and gold across Sommer's skin.

Naked, Sommer bent and reached for something on the floor, out of Dean's sight. He came up with a huge tub of vegetable shortening, which Dean realized must've come from the kitchen. Dean let out a snort.

"Hey, I do a lot of baking," Sommer said, laughing along with Dean. "All my shortening tubs are this size."

Dean grinned. "Please tell me you're not gonna use that for cooking after this."

"Oh sure. My ass-flavored biscuits are super popular."

While Dean was still shaking with laughter, Sommer knelt between his legs, caressing his thighs. "Are you ready?"

Dean sobered instantly. He gazed up into Sommer's warm brown eyes, heart racing. "Yeah. Ready."

Taking another towel from a small stack on the mattress, Sommer folded one and tapped it against Dean's ass. Dean obediently lifted his hips so Sommer could slide the folded towel underneath them. Pelvis thus tilted up, Dean hooked his hands behind his knees and lifted his legs up and apart.

"Mmmm. There's that pretty little hole." Eyes blazing, Sommer removed the lid from the can of shortening, scooped some onto his fingers and reached between Dean's buttocks. A thickly greased finger rubbed firm circles across Dean's anus before slipping inside him. Dean moaned, and Sommer smiled, pushing a second finger into Dean's ass. "That's it. Open up for me."

Dean lost track of how much time passed while Sommer patiently worked him open. It could have been minutes, or hours, or even days. He didn't know, and didn't care. Having given himself into Sommer's keeping, time no longer mattered. Every nerve in his body hummed and sparked in response to Sommer's touch. He never wanted it to end.

Drunk on sensation, mind and body singing, Dean wondered if he and Sommer had fallen out of the stream of time completely. If maybe they'd spend the rest of eternity just like this, Dean spread and exposed, Sommer's clever fingers sending him flying.

I wish we could. I don't want to lose this, not ever.

Between Dean's legs, the slow massage of Sommer's fingers gave way to a feeling of steady pressure. Dean's consciousness snapped into sharp focus. "Sommer..."

"Yes." Leaning sideways, Sommer kissed the inside of Dean's ankle. "Breathe, beautiful. Let me in."

Dean drew a deep breath and blew it out. His body relaxed, and Sommer's hand slid slowly through the ring of muscle and into his ass.

"Oh God," Dean whispered, fingers digging into the backs of his thighs as his hole stretched to accommodate the width of Sommer's knuckles. "God, yes. Oh."

Sommer's gaze flicked from Dean's face to his ass and back again, features taut with concentration and dark eyes molten with desire. His hand pushed into Dean in one slow, smooth motion. Dean's mouth opened in a nearly silent gasp of pleasure at the feel of Sommer's long fingers folding into a fist inside him.

"God, you feel good inside," Sommer murmured. He stilled, keeping his hand motionless. "So alive."

If Dean could've formed words at that point, he would've agreed. He could feel his hole pulsing around Sommer's wrist, adjusting to the intrusion. Unable to speak, Dean communicated his pleasure with a series of soft little "oh, oh, oh" sounds.

"Gonna move now," Sommer whispered. "Okay?"

Dean nodded. "Please," he rasped, forming the word

with an effort.

Wrapping his free hand around Dean's cock, he gave the fist in Dean's ass a gentle twist. Dean moaned and spread himself wider. Nothing had ever felt as amazing as Sommer's hand in him, filling him up and caressing his insides.

A tiny coherent part of Dean's brain knew this would be a one-time experience. That part of him mourned the coming loss of something he'd only just realized he wanted to keep.

Thankfully, the vast majority of his mind was occupied with processing the overwhelming tide of sensation washing through his body. It made it easier to ignore the less-than-welcome realization of exactly what he felt for Sommer.

When Sommer's hand began pumping inside him, moving in tiny pulses which sent shockwaves shooting through him, Dean couldn't hold out any longer. "Ooooh, oh God," he wailed, hips canting upward and eyes fluttering closed. "Sommer..."

"Yeah." Sommer's grip on Dean's prick tightened, thumb nudging the plug enough to send electric jolts shooting up Dean's shaft. Inside his ass, Sommer's hand corkscrewed, hitting his prostate and tearing a keening cry from him. "Open your eyes, beautiful. Look at me."

Forcing his eyes open, Dean focused on Sommer's face. Sommer's gaze caught and held his. The look in Sommer's eyes, both lustful and tender, sent Dean spinning over the precipice into an orgasm so intense it squeezed the breath from his lungs. His back arched, fingers digging into his thighs with bruising force as his insides rippled around Sommer's hand. Semen splashed thick and hot on his belly.

Through sex-blurred vision, Dean saw Sommer's lips quirk into *that* smile, the one that made Dean feel giddy and feverish. "I wish you could see yourself right now," Sommer murmured, his voice soft and dreamy. "You look incredible with your legs up and my hand in your ass, and come all over you."

Dean let out a hoarse laugh, which morphed into a wavering moan when Sommer eased his hand carefully out of Dean's hole. "I probably look the same way I feel. Thoroughly fucked."

"Mm. You do, actually." Sommer pried Dean's fingers off the backs of his thighs and helped him lower his legs to the bed. Picking up an extra towel, Sommer wiped the liquefied shortening off his hand. "Just looking at you like this makes me want to come."

Dean reached up to caress Sommer's cheek. The way Sommer leaned into the touch tugged at his heart. "What do you want, Sommer? You want my mouth, or my hand?" He flashed a wicked grin. "I'd give you my ass, but—"

"No condoms. Dammit."

"Nope." Hooking his hand around the back of Sommer's neck, Dean pulled his face down to kiss him. "So what do you want?" Dean ran his tongue across Sommer's parted lips, licking up the taste of sweat and need. "I'm your slut, Sommer. You can do anything you want to me."

A solemn expression came over Sommer's face. Pressing himself between Dean's splayed legs, Sommer laid a kiss on his brow. "Don't say that. You're not."

Dean wanted to ask if that meant he wasn't a slut, or wasn't Sommer's. Or both. But Sommer's tongue pushed into his mouth, and he didn't have the heart to stop him in order to ask. He wasn't sure he wanted to know anyway. Closing his eyes, Dean wrapped both legs around Sommer's waist and opened his mouth wide.

It didn't take long for Sommer to finish. His hips rocked into Dean's, his cock sliding against Dean's grease-slick groin. When he came, he breathed a soft cry into Dean's mouth. His lips moved, forming silent words Dean felt but didn't understand. Dean held him in arms and legs, stroking his damp hair and trembling back.

He bit back the declaration which wanted to come out. He didn't trust it, no matter how right it felt.

People don't fall in love this fast, he reminded himself, as Sommer collapsed at his side and drew him into his arms. *You think you love him because of what all you've shared this past month, and what you just did together. You can't do all that with someone and not feel a connection. That's all it is.*

Looking into Sommer's shining eyes, he knew he was lying to himself. But there was no choice, really. Even if what he felt was real, the reality of it was that even the strongest love faded with time and distance. Something this new and fragile would never survive long months and hundreds of miles of separation.

He'd had his heart broken before, and he'd survived. He could survive it again.

Sommer's hand touched his cheek. "What are you thinking?"

Dean nuzzled into Sommer's palm, catching his own scent mixed with the smell of vegetable grease and sweat. "Nothing," he lied. He felt a familiar smile—the evil, teasing one he liked to hide behind—spread over his face. "Reckon we have time for one more before you have to take me home?"

Sommer looked startled, then burst out laughing. "Good grief, you're horny."

"Guilty." Tightening his grip on Sommer's body, Dean tilted his head to kiss Sommer's lips. "Let me suck your cock. I didn't get to finish you off before."

Sommer's low groan was answer enough. His hand fisted into Dean's hair, drawing him into one of those consuming, mind-blowing kisses.

Dean gladly opened to him. Neither of them was hard yet, but it was only a matter of time. And as long as they were working together toward the common goal of getting off one more time, Dean didn't have to think about falling in love with someone he'd never see again.

Chapter Fifteen

Two hours later, Sommer's SUV pulled up in Kerry and Ron's driveway. Dean unbuckled his seat belt and sat twisting his fingers together, wondering if he'd ever felt so awkward. Finally facing up to his feelings for Sommer had changed things. He knew he couldn't see Sommer again, not unless there was a chance for them to be together. And he knew there was no chance.

Beside him, Sommer drummed his fingers against the steering wheel and stared moodily out the windshield. "Sorry you couldn't stay tonight."

"Yeah. I hate it, but my flight's at seven a.m., so I'll need to get up about four thirty." That, at least, was true. Not that such a thing would normally have stopped him from spending one more night with Sommer. But he couldn't face the pain of being with Sommer, knowing he was in love with the man and would never see him again. Best to end it now. "Sorry."

Sommer shrugged. "It's okay."

Dean bit his lip. "I'll call you," he said, and instantly wished he hadn't. He wasn't going to call, and he knew it.

Judging by the bitter smile curving Sommer's mouth,

he knew it too. "Yeah."

"So. I guess I should go."

"Yeah."

They stared at each other. Dean wished he could read Sommer's mind, to know what the man felt right now. Was he feeling as torn apart as Dean, or was he glad he was leaving? Dean couldn't tell, and he hated that. Even more, he hated that he didn't have the balls to just ask, because he didn't want to see that careful, "I-don't-want-to-hurt-you-but..." look in Sommer's eyes.

You're overthinking again, stupid. It doesn't matter anymore. Kiss him, say goodbye and get out of the fucking car.

With an impatient growl, Dean reached over and yanked Sommer's face to his. He grabbed a handful of Sommer's hair, still damp from the shower they'd taken together, and kissed him hard. Sommer opened to him with a sigh, one hand sliding behind his head.

The kiss was deep and languid, warm and wet and brimming with all the things Dean was too afraid to say, and too afraid to believe Sommer might feel as well. It was a kiss Dean could take with him, keep in his heart and draw out for comfort on cold nights alone in his bed.

He wished it could go on forever, that time could halt right here and just let him keep this feeling. But life didn't work that way. Eventually, the kiss broke. Dean closed his eyes and rested his forehead against Sommer's.

"What are you thinking?" Sommer asked, lifting Dean's face with a finger under his chin.

"I was thinking I wish I could stay." Dean opened his eyes again, his gaze meeting Sommer's. "But I can't."

Sommer's eyes darkened with a loneliness so deep it tore at Dean's soul. Then he smiled his crooked smile, and the loneliness was masked once more. "I know. I wish you could stay too."

Something in his voice told Dean that Sommer didn't mean he wished he could stay just for a day.

For one blazing second, Dean trembled on the razor's edge, caught between what he already had and what he desperately wanted. But in the end, he didn't have the courage to throw away everything he knew and loved for something that might not even exist.

With one final kiss, light and chaste, he pulled away, got out of the SUV and walked up to Ron and Kerry's door. He didn't look back.

♥

"Call me when you get home."

"I will."

"And be sure to email me your pictures. I'll send you mine too."

"Sure thing."

Grabbing Dean's arm, Kerry stopped them halfway between the ticket counter and the security checkpoint of the Raleigh-Durham airport, where Dean had just checked in for his flight home. "Dean, I know I keep asking this, but are you okay?"

Dean forced a smile. "Yeah, I'm fine."

"Uh-huh. Sure you are." Planting her free hand on her hip, she gave him a stern look. "Ever since you left Sommer's place yesterday, you've been acting like your favorite uncle died or something. You think you're hiding it, and you've successfully avoided talking about it until now, but you can't fool me. Now tell me what happened."

Sighing, Dean shook his head. "It doesn't matter."

"It matters to me."

"It doesn't to me."

"Liar." Kerry shook his arm, her blue eyes full of worry. "Dean, talk to me. What did he do to you?"

Dean stared at the red duct tape holding the handle of his ancient carry-on bag together. "He didn't do anything. I just..." *I fell in love without meaning to, even though it was a stupid thing to do, then I left because I was fucking scared.* "I don't know. I can't explain, Kerry. I'm sorry."

Kerry's eyes narrowed, and Dean's stomach rolled. If she guessed what he really felt, she'd never leave it alone. She might even go talk to Sommer, which would be a disaster.

Would it really? What if he decided all he needed to be happy was you? What if he left Chapel Hill for you, and you could be together for real?

Dean shook himself, forcing the hopeful little voice into the back of his mind where it belonged. It was a nice fantasy, but that's all it was. Those things didn't happen in real life.

"I gotta go," Dean said, glancing at his watch to prove his point. "My flight'll be boarding in a little while."

For a moment, Kerry looked ready to argue. Then she shook her head, stood on tiptoe and wound both arms around his neck. "Bye, Dean. Have a good trip."

"I will." He hugged her tight, then pulled away and kissed her cheek. "Love you."

"Love you too." Taking his hand, she gave it a hard squeeze. "Don't forget to call."

"I won't." He let her hand fall from his. "Bye."

She gave him a watery smile, eyes suspiciously red, then turned and walked briskly toward the terminal door. He watched her until she was out of sight.

Grasping the handle of his bag, he went to join the line at the security checkpoint. He wished going through the metal arch to the gates didn't feel so damn final.

Soft moans. Deep, hungry kisses. Hands on his body, hard cock fucking him slow and sweet. Brown eyes aglow, silky hair brushing his face. A whispered "I love you," and it was everything he'd ever wanted...

A hand nudged Dean's shoulder, jarring him from his fantasy. He blinked up at his coworker and friend, Sam Raintree, who stood frowning at him. "Sorry, Sam. I zoned out."

"I'll say." Easing into the chair at the desk beside Dean's, Sam gave him a worried look. "Is everything all right? You've been out of sorts ever since you got back from Chapel Hill."

Dean faked a smile. "I'm fine. Just been kind of tired lately, that's all. It's probably just a cold or something."

Sam didn't look convinced at all, but he nodded. "Why don't you go on home? I can finish up your research for you."

Dean grimaced. He'd much rather stay here in the back room of the Bay City Paranormal Investigations office, up to his neck in research, than face the empty hours alone in his tiny apartment. Especially now, on Valentine's Day. A day meant for lovers.

He'd hoped two weeks would be long enough to show him he didn't *really* love Sommer after all. All it had shown him was how irretrievably he'd fallen. No way could he face Valentine's Day alone with memories, wishes and his own cowardice.

"No thanks," Dean answered, trying to sound casual. "I'm fine, honest. I like doing research."

Crossing his arms, Sam arched a skeptical brow at him. "Okay. If you say so."

"I do say so." Dean laid a hand on Sam's arm. "Thanks for being worried about me, though. It's kind of nice."

"What are friends for?" Smiling, Sam ruffled Dean's hair and moved back to the other desk in the back room, where he was writing a report of their latest investigation. "Let me know if you change your mind."

Dean nodded and waved Sam away with a smile.

Sam's concern was endearing, and comforting. It was nice to know he could talk to Sam—or, in fact, any of his friends at BCPI—about what had happened with Sommer. He wasn't ready to do that yet, but knowing they would listen helped tremendously.

Shaking his head at his own pathetic behavior, Dean turned back to his computer. He had work to do.

♥

The day wore on, the individual minutes ticking away hour after busy hour. Bay City Paranormal had picked up three new cases since Dean had returned from his trip, and they'd all been working nonstop ever since. Dean was glad of it. Sommer stayed on his mind constantly, but he hadn't had time to dwell on thoughts of the man, and all that had and had not happened between them.

Okay, so he'd lost himself in romantic fantasies a couple of times. They hadn't lasted long, and Dean was determined that it wouldn't happen again.

At the next desk over, Sam yawned and stretched. "Is it time to leave yet?"

Dean glanced at the red plastic clock sitting on the empty desk next to his. "Four thirty. But you and Bo have been here since, what, seven?"

"Mm-hm." Sam yawned again and rubbed his hands over his face. "Damn. Okay, I think I'll go see if I can talk Bo into leaving a little early."

Dean grinned. "Entice him with sex, and he'll do

whatever you want."

Sam turned red, and Dean laughed in spite of his lingering sadness. Sam and Dr. Bo Broussard, founder of Bay City Paranormal, had been lovers for over a year now, and Sam still seemed to regard that fact with wonder. Dean thought it was adorable.

"We thought we'd drive across the bay to Rousso's for dinner. I'd kind of like to beat the Valentine's crowd." In the front room of the office, the squeak of the door announced the arrival of a visitor. Sam rolled his chair over to the door into the other room and peeked out. "Dammit, I hope this isn't another case. We're covered up as it is."

"True." Pushing himself out of the chair, Dean pressed both palms to the small of his back and arched his spine. Sitting at a computer all day was hell on his back. "So I take it whoever's here isn't anyone we already know?" The sound of murmured voices drifted from the other room.

"No. At least I've never seen him before." Sam flashed a wicked grin. "He's pretty hot, though. You could give it a try."

Dean snorted. "What if he's not into guys?"

"Dean, you could turn the straightest man on the planet."

Snickering, Dean leaned over to thump Sam on the shoulder.

"Dean?"

He looked up to see Danica McClellan, BCPI's

receptionist and general office manager, standing in the doorway. "Yeah?"

"There's someone here to see you." Glancing behind her, she dropped her voice to a near-whisper. "He says the two of you met in Chapel Hill, and he's anxious to talk to you. He's acting a bit strange, though. Would you like me to tell him you're busy?"

Dean barely registered anything after the words "met in Chapel Hill". He felt like he'd been kicked in the stomach.

It can't be him. It can't. Those things don't happen.

A hand slid around his wrist. "Dean, you don't look so good," Sam said, brow furrowed. "Why don't you sit down?"

"I'll tell your visitor he'll have to call another time," Danny added. "And then I'll bring you some tea."

"No, wait." Lunging forward, Dean grabbed Danny's arm before she could leave. She raised her eyebrows at him. He drew a deep breath and let it out slowly, trying to calm his racing pulse. "It's okay. I'll...I'll come talk to him."

She looked dubious. "All right, if you're certain."

"I'm sure," Dean said, feeling anything but. Steeling himself, he forced his legs to move, to carry him into the front room.

And there he was. Right there on the other side of Danny's desk. Sommer Skye.

Chapter Sixteen

Dean's vision tunneled, blotting out everything but the sight of Sommer standing there in faded jeans and a UNC sweater, long fingers twisting nervously together. God, he looked good. A rush of longing turned Dean's knees to jelly.

"Sommer." Dean's voice shook. He cleared his throat and tried again. "What are you...? I mean, I didn't expect..." He fell silent, staring at Sommer's mouth because he was afraid to look into his eyes. Afraid, because what he saw there might not be what he wanted to see.

"I, um, I was in town, and I remembered you said you worked here, and I just... I thought I'd..." Sommer bit his lip. "Could we go someplace and talk?"

Dean blinked. For a moment, he'd completely forgotten where he was. He glanced sideways, taking in Sam and Danny's stunned expressions. Behind Sommer, the rest of the BCPI employees stood huddled together, staring at the two of them in cautious silence.

Dean licked his dry lips, watching Sommer watch the movement of his tongue. "Um. Yeah. Good idea." Running a trembling hand through his hair, he glanced at his boss. "Okay if I take off, Bo?"

Bo nodded, dark eyes curious. "Of course."

"'Kay. Thanks." Grabbing Sommer's wrist, Dean dragged him toward the front door. He flung it open, strode out onto the porch with Sommer's wrist in a death grip, and shut the door behind him.

They were already in Dean's lime green Civic before Dean realized he hadn't even introduced Sommer to his friends. He grimaced, irritated with himself. *Oh well, I can always do it later. I hope.*

Dean cranked the engine and backed out into the Dauphin Street traffic. He narrowly avoided being sideswiped by a gleaming black Ford pickup. The truck's horn blared with what Dean swore was an accusatory tone.

With a sheepish smile, Dean glanced at Sommer, who was gripping the seat so hard his knuckles were white. "Sorry. It's just...I didn't expect to see you. Here, I mean." *Or anywhere, ever, and God did that hurt.*

"I know." Turning sideways as much as possible in his seat belt, Sommer stared at Dean with worried eyes. "I hope I haven't just made a horrible mistake."

Dean reached over and laid his hand over Sommer's. "Whatever the reason is for your being here, it's not a mistake."

He wasn't sure he'd feel the same if Sommer spent a night or two in his bed then left, but for now he meant what he'd said. Sommer was here, right here beside him, and he intended to seize the moment. To let Sommer erase the ache inside him, even if it was only for a few hours.

Sommer didn't answer, but his lips curved into the lopsided smile which always set Dean's heart thumping. Staring at that sweet, oh-so-kissable mouth, Dean nearly ran off the road.

"Let's go to The Back Porch," he suggested, once the shock of almost wrecking for the second time in less than five minutes had worn off. "It's close by, the red beans and rice is out of this world and the tables are really private."

"Sounds good to me." Sommer twisted his hand beneath Dean's and wound their fingers together. "I have a lot to tell you, and I'd rather do it someplace where surprising you won't get us both killed."

Dean laughed, feeling a thousand pounds lighter than he had in the last two weeks. He didn't know what sort of "surprises" Sommer had in store, but nothing could stop him from hoping for things he hadn't dared consider before Sommer walked back into his life.

The drive to The Back Porch took only a few minutes. Dean found an empty space in the back of the oyster-shell parking lot, and he and Sommer hurried inside to escape the damp February chill. Dean stuck his hands under his armpits, berating himself for leaving his jacket at the office in his hurry to get out.

"This is cute," Sommer said after they'd put their names on the list and settled themselves in the small parlor which served as a waiting area. "Is this whole place the restaurant?"

Dean nodded. "This house has been here more than a hundred years. The original owners lived here in the house and ran a small restaurant on the back porch."

"Thus the name, right?"

"Right. It was expanded in the fifties to include the whole house, and here it's been ever since. They have a brief history of the place on the back of the menu." Scooting closer, Dean laid a hand on Sommer's knee. "Sommer, why are you here? Is this just a visit, or..."

He couldn't finish. Sommer took his hand, raised it to his mouth and kissed it. That smile, shy but *not* shy, spread over Sommer's face, and a wild hope leapt in Dean's chest.

"It's not a visit." Sommer's voice was soft but sure. "I spoke with a realtor, and I've rented an apartment a couple of miles from here. I moved in this morning. I'm starting a new job as a manager in a local wine shop in a couple of weeks."

Dean swallowed a couple of times before he could speak. "You... What? You did *what*?"

"I left Chapel Hill, and moved here." Sommer's smile faded, apprehension rising in his eyes. "I...I thought—"

"You thought right," Dean interrupted, hating to see Sommer's uncertainty. "God, I missed you. I'm so happy you're here."

Sommer's relief was palpable. He leaned closer. "Dean, I—"

"Delapore, table for two?"

The hostess's high, clear voice made Dean jump. He gave Sommer a look to say their conversation wasn't over, then stood and pulled Sommer up with him.

They followed the hostess to a small round table tucked into a cozy corner of the upstairs back room. The dim lamplight revealed pale pine floors and walls painted a deep forest green. Little glass-covered candles sat on each of the room's four tables. Strategically placed standing screens gave every table a feeling of privacy. Beside Dean and Sommer's table, a large bay window overlooked a narrow side street shaded by live oaks and lined with neat Victorian cottages.

A waitress was at their side before they'd even sat down, offering drinks and menus. Sommer ordered something which sounded French. Dean couldn't have pronounced it if he'd tried, but he figured it must be wine since Sommer seemed so confident about what he was ordering.

Dean waited until the bottle had been fetched and opened—it *was* wine, something deep red with a spicy scent that made him want to sneeze—before he started asking questions. As soon as Sommer had pronounced the wine acceptable and the waitress had taken their dinner orders, Dean braced himself to learn the story behind Sommer's sudden arrival.

"What did you do with your place?" he asked, that question being the most pressing other than the one he was still half-afraid to ask. Starting off with *do you love me like I love you* probably wasn't a great idea, so best to begin with the easy ones.

Picking up his glass, Sommer took a sip of wine. "I sold it."

Dean blinked. "You sold it?"

"Yeah. Or rather, it's on the market. It's not sold yet, but there's a couple of folks in the area who've had their eyes on it for a while now. I think I'll get a fair offer."

"Why?" Dean couldn't believe what he was hearing. Had Sommer sold his house and his business and moved several hundred miles for his own reasons, or for the chance to be with Dean?

God, I hope he didn't do it just for me. He didn't think he could shoulder the full responsibility for that degree of upheaval in Sommer's life.

Sommer shrugged. "Because you were right when you said I didn't like it there. I didn't. I mean, Chapel Hill's a great town, and I loved the winemaking part of it, but I hated the business side of things. Plus I was terrible at it. I've been wanting out for a while, actually." Sommer stared out the window for a moment before meeting Dean's gaze again. "I've been thinking about it, and I think that's one reason I was so upset when you suggested that my mother was dead. Part of me has been waiting all this time for her and Dad to come back and take the load of the business off my back."

Not knowing what to say to that, Dean took Sommer's hand and gave it a comforting squeeze. Sommer gave him a faint smile in return.

"I saw this as a perfect chance to make the changes

I've been needing in my life," Sommer continued, watching Dean's face. "A chance to follow my heart for once."

Something deep in Dean's gut pulled tight. Relief that Sommer's decision hadn't been entirely about him? Fear— or possibly excitement—over what was in Sommer's heart to lead him here?

Dean wasn't sure. Nor was he sure he was ready for the answer, so he ignored the implications in Sommer's words. "What about the body? Did they find out for sure if it's your mom?"

"The DNA tests will take a while to come back, but I know it's her. I can feel it." The corner of Sommer's mouth hitched up. "I never told you this, but you remember that EVP we caught, the first time we saw the ghost in the upstairs room? I thought I recognized my mother's voice. I dismissed it at the time, figuring it was just my imagination. But looking back, I guess I knew it was her even then. I'm sorry I gave you such shit about it."

It warmed Dean's heart that Sommer would still feel guilty about their fight, but he didn't want Sommer to continue beating himself up over something Dean had long since put behind him. "Don't worry about it. That's ancient history now." He gave Sommer a reassuring smile. "So, have they been able to figure out how your mom died? Was it her cancer? I mean, you don't have to talk about it if you don't want, but you know you can, right?"

Turning his hand in Dean's, Sommer laced their fingers together. "I know, and I appreciate that more than I can tell you. To answer your question, they can't pinpoint an exact cause yet, but they believe she died of natural causes."

Tilting his head, Dean gave Sommer a cautious look. "Then it must've been your dad who buried her, like you said before."

"Most likely." Sommer leaned forward, his voice dropping low. "When I was growing up they always talked about a natural burial. Just being put in the ground, without embalming or coffins or anything. Which is probably illegal." He smiled, and it was a sad smile this time. "I can see my father doing that. Burying her the way she wanted, without even a grave marker, then just leaving everything behind. He always was a hopeless romantic."

"I don't see what's romantic about burying your wife and then leaving, without even telling anyone—including your *son*, for fuck's sake—what happened." Dean grimaced, angry on Sommer's behalf. "That's just fucked up."

"Yeah, but he wouldn't have seen it that way." Sommer took another sip of wine, licking the residue from his lips in a way Dean found enchanting. "Maybe that's not even what happened. It doesn't matter anyway. What's done is done. I have to move on now. I have to live my own life, for myself, and for...for the people I love."

Oh God, this is it. Heart nearly pounding through his rib cage, Dean stared into Sommer's eyes. "You were about to say something, before the hostess called us. What was it?"

Sommer drew a deep breath and let it out slowly. "I

know we haven't known each other long, but I..." He bit his lip, brown eyes glittering in the lamplight. His free hand came up to cup Dean's cheek. When he spoke again, his voice was a raw whisper. "I love you, Dean. It's crazy, I know, but I do."

He loves me. The tense bubble in Dean's gut burst, sending a wave of euphoria washing over him. Beaming, he surged forward and planted a hard kiss on Sommer's mouth.

"I'm so fucking glad you said that," he murmured as he drew back. "Because I've known I was in love with you since the minute you stuck your hand up my ass."

Sommer let out a startled laugh, palm dropping from Dean's cheek. His other hand remained tangled with Dean's. "You sure have a way with words."

"That's what they tell me." Feeling playful, Dean picked up his wineglass and arched an eyebrow at Sommer over the rim. "Of course, no one ever says if my way is good or bad."

"Definitely good." Sommer grinned, pure joy glowing in his face. "God, I'm relieved. I was a nervous wreck coming here, not knowing for sure what you'd say."

"But you came here anyway." Dean shook his head. "You're a brave man, Sommer. I never would've had the guts to leave my home like that, not knowing what would happen."

"It wasn't so brave, really." Sommer laid two fingers over Dean's mouth, cutting off his protest. "They say home is where the heart is. Chapel Hill and the Blue Skye

Inn stopped being my home the minute you left."

Warmth blossomed in Dean's chest. He couldn't speak past the emotion clogging his throat, but Sommer seemed to understand exactly how he felt. Leaning forward at the same time, they came together in a soft, slow kiss which said it all.

When they pulled apart, Dean smiled. "Welcome home."

About the Author

Ally Blue is acknowledged by the world at large (or at least by her heroes, who tend to suffer a lot) as the Popess of Gay Angst. She has a great big penis hat and rides in a bullet-proof Plexiglas bubble in Christmas parades. Her harem of manwhores does double duty as bodyguards and sinspirational entertainment. Her favorite band is Radiohead, her favorite color is lime green and her favorite way to waste a perfectly good Saturday is to watch all three extended version LOTR movies in a row. Her ultimate dream is to one day ditch the evil day job and support the family on manlove alone. She is not a hippie or a brain surgeon, no matter what her kids' friends say.

To learn more about Ally Blue, please visit www.allyblue.com. Send an email to Ally at ally@allyblue.com or join her Yahoo! group to join in the fun with other readers as well as Ally! http://groups.yahoo.com/group/loveisblue/.

The time has come for Kir to use his powers to destroy the agency and bring Josh back to safety.

Minder
© *2007 Joely Skye*

Third book of the Minders series

Josh goes to ground after being given the compulsion to kill his lover. But the agency ensures Josh is not the only threat to Kir's life.

Last summer, Kir arrived home to blood and death. Josh was gone. All Kir has left is his belief Josh is still alive. Until the agency entraps Kir and suddenly Josh is back in his life. But Josh is not the same man who disappeared almost a year ago...

Josh knows how to kill. Kir, a Minder, can bend people to his will. They will each have to act to keep the other safe, no matter the cost.

Warning: This title contains explicit male/male sex. Due to the serial nature of these stories, the author recommends reading the series in order.

Available now in ebook from Samhain Publishing.
Also available in the print anthology Beautiful Monster from Samhain Publishing.

GREAT CHEAP FUN

Discover eBooks!

THE FASTEST WAY TO GET THE HOTTEST NAMES

Get your favorite authors on your favorite reader, long before they're
out in print! Ebooks from Samhain go wherever you go, and work with
whatever you carry—Palm, PDF, Mobi, and more.

WWW.SAMHAINPUBLISHING.COM

LaVergne, TN USA
28 September 2009
159246LV00003B/49/P